ONCE UPON A TIME IN THE FUTURE

Cinch's slug took Brilly high on the right side of the chest, almost at the shoulder. It didn't look like a fatal wound, no major organs there, but it put him down. The thug started yelling, cursing. Cinch moved forward to help the wounded man.

The spring dog beat him there.

Cinch emptied the rest of the magazine at the dog, but it was a waste of time and ammo. Apparently somebody had overriden its visual-attack-only program. There was nothing in the universe that could save Brilly. The sound of human flesh and bones being torn and crunched filled the night.

Brilly stopped cursing.

STELLAR RANGER

STEVE PERRY

AVON BOOKS • NEW YORK

STELLAR RANGER is an original publication of Avon Books. This work has never before appeared in book form. This work is a novel. Any similarity to actual persons or events is purely coincidental.

AVON BOOKS
A division of
The Hearst Corporation
1350 Avenue of the Americas
New York, New York 10019

Copyright © 1994 by Bill Fawcett and Associates
Cover art by Dorian Vallejo
Published by arrangement with Bill Fawcett and Associates
Library of Congress Catalog Card Number: 93-90820
ISBN: 0-380-77301-5

First AvoNova Printing: May 1994

AVONOVA TRADEMARK REG. U.S. PAT. OFF. AND IN OTHER COUNTRIES, MARCA REGISTRADA, HECHO EN U.S.A.

Printed in the U.S.A.

RA 10 9 8 7 6 5 4 3 2 1

This one is for Dianne;
And for the aunts: Anabelle,
Tootsie, Barbara and Linda.

Wherever Law ends, Tyranny begins.
—John Locke

chapter 1

Something nasty had killed Gustav Kohl's prize stud bull.

Cinch Carston squatted on his heels next to what was left of the bull, looking for clues. Not that there was much left to see. The remains of the entrails had been sun-cooked to stringy, gelid ropes, most of the hindquarters eaten here or dragged and consumed a short way off. Dried blood trails smeared the dirt, thicker near the remains, dribbling to brown flecks only a few meters away. The front half of the critter had also been attended to, the skull and horns and a few vertebrae left behind, those already beginning to bleach under Roget's hot summer sunshine. Along with a few late-hatched maggots, flies, and that sickly sweet rotten-meat stink, that was pretty much it.

Cinch rose from his crouch and slowly backed away, reusing his own tracks in the sandy soil to avoid disturbing any possible clues. A few of the flies startled and buzzed, not many.

The vegetation was sparse here on the plain—scraggly bushes and some short Terran grasses that had taken during the planet's seeding. There was little water hereabouts; it was hot most of the days, cold at night. Good for running cattle and raising blueweed and not much else. Just like half a dozen frontier planets he'd seen before.

Cinch shoved his hat back a little with his thumb and

continued to look at the bull's carcass. He didn't much like what he saw. Or smelled, for that.

From behind him Kohl said, "I don't know how the hell Tuluk managed to train the damned ularsinga to attack my cattle."

Cinch took one last look at the kill, then turned to face the speaker.

Kohl was probably thirty years older than the ranger, an easy eighty-five standards. In a galaxy where a man who took care of himself could expect to reach a hundred and thirty, that made the rancher a couple of decades past middle age, Cinch still half that much short of it. But he was a tough one, Kohl, his face seamed and leathery from the weather on this world, his hair white under the wide-brimmed hat he wore for shade. Like many on the frontier tropical or desert worlds, Kohl couldn't be bothered to use sunblock or melanin implants. He probably had to go in every year or so and have the skin cancers blistered from his face and hands. Cinch would bet the rest of the older man was as pale as new snow under his long-sleeved polypropyl shirt and synlin pants. Sweat stained the cloth, evaporating quickly in the dry heat. Not yet noon and already the temperature out here was well above body heat. Couple more hours and it would be really hot. Cook your brain without a hat. Cinch sometimes wondered if he'd gone hatless too many times already. His own hat and clothes were all that protected him from the fierce sun that beat down on them. He hardly bothered with sunblock himself. When you worked with locals, it didn't help if you looked as light as a ghost. That marked you as somebody who didn't get outside much. Frontier folk saw a tan, they sometimes mistook you for one of their own kind.

"It wasn't ularsinga killed this animal," Cinch said. He'd done the requisite scans of the background info when he'd made the hop to this world. The older man was talking about the local predator, an alligatorlike land lizard that normally fed on smaller game like rabbits and ground squirrels. Some of the ularsinga—the name meant "lion snake" in the local lingo—ran to four and half meters in length and maybe a hundred and sixty kilos. They were, according to the scans, faster than a man for short distances and capable of bringing down a full-grown beef cow, especially when they hunted in pairs or triplets as they sometimes did.

Kohl blinked at Cinch. "I'm not one to try to tell a Stellar Ranger his bidness, but a half-blind idiot can see the lizard track and scat all over the place."

Cinch nodded. That was true enough. And the lizard shit stank worse than the carcass. "Yep. The ularsinga surely were here and they did eat most of the bull but it was dead when they got to it." He turned back toward the carcass. "Come look at this."

With both men squatting on the ground, Cinch pointed at the base of the bull's skull. A local beetle crawled over the bone. God must like beetles, he made so many of them. Anywhere men lived, beetles showed up eventually. "See the vertebra, right there?"

" 'Course I can see it."

"Look at the marks, there and there."

"I ain't blind, son. What am I looking at here?"

"When a predator with sharp teeth bites something, it leaves marks like that. Usually, though, they look more like those over there." He pointed at a gnawed shoulder blade half a meter from the skull. "No matter how sharp they are, natural teeth are still biologically generated enamel. Harder than wet bone, but not all that much, relatively speaking."

"Okay, son, I appreciate the dental lecture. Get to it."

Cinch grinned at the older man's impatience. "The marks on the backbone are sharp-edged, clean, much deeper and fewer than those on the other bones."

"Which means?"

"Whatever chewed through this animal's neck did it fast and hard. I can't tell without putting it under the scope, but my guess is I'll find metal molecules on the cuts, probably durasteel or titanium."

"You're saying it was cut?"

"No, sir. It was bitten through, all right, but by something with steel teeth and jaws a lot more powerful than your local lizards—even on a real good day. No natural predator on this planet could do it."

"Sweet Baby Jesus and Buddha in a Hammock," Kohl said.

Kohl piloted the two-seater GE car. Cinch sat next to him and looked at the sage as the car zipped across the flat ground. They left a dusty wake behind them. Most of his gear was stowed at the port, but he'd brought a few things. He could confirm his idea about the bone easy enough, he had collected the vertebrae in a padded silicone bag for the analysis. Though he and Kohl had walked the surrounding area looking for more tracks, the wind and scavengers had obliterated any such sign. It would have helped to find prints, but they hadn't and that was that.

The airwall kept enough wind and motor sound out of the topless car so they could hear each other when they spoke, if they raised their voices to a near-shout. The stray dust that found its way into the car was gritty and had a faint alkali taste.

Cinch spat. "Tell me about Tuluk," he said.

"Not much to tell. He's richer than God, owns the biggest blueweed field west of the Impossibles, runs a hundred thousand head of cattle, most of 'em prime cross-breed *zait*-stock—that's green beeves and going for thirteen a kilo before freezing, right at the moment. It ain't enough for him, though, he wants to own *all* the cattle on the planet, all the blueweed, and everything else he can get his clammy hands on. He's a greedy son of a bitch."

Cinch nodded. That wasn't quite how the scans had put it, but Manis Tuluk was listed as the richest man on the planet of Roget, the wealth not inherited. In his experience, most very rich people who had come by their money through their own efforts had a certain kind of mind-set. True, there were inventors who discovered some new principle or device that could shower them with accidental fortunes, but the people who earned their way into riches by running cattle and growing crops didn't do it by accident. . . .

Cinch's mentation cut off when something *spanged* into

the side of the car close to his right hip. He felt the tug as whatever it was tore through the seat a centimeter behind his lower back. The *crack* of the sound followed almost immediately. Hormones surged through the ranger like a tsunami, washing his insides into a gut-twisting reaction.

"Turn!" Cinch commanded. "Get off the road!"

Gustav Kohl did not hesitate. He twisted the control wheel to the left. The car swerved from the packed dirt road and flew a half meter high over the looser sandy topsoil of the empty field. The GE fans blew great clouds of red-brown dust into the air, a natural screen that hid the car from behind. Or so Cinch hoped.

"Swerve back and forth," Cinch said. "Kick up as much dust as you can."

The ranger already had his pistol out, looking for a target, but the cloud behind them worked both ways. If the shooter couldn't see them, neither could he see the shooter. Not that he was likely to hit anything at this range. There was a stand of trees maybe five hundred meters on the other side of the road, the only spot big enough to hide an assassin and his vehicle, and he surely wasn't on foot way out here. From the trees, he'd have a difficult shot at a fast-moving target even with a dot-scoped target rifle. And that far away, Cinch wasn't going to be doing a lot of damage himself. The bullet would reach that distance, in theory, but hitting a man-sized object was real iffy. But it was what he had. He held the antique Smith in both hands, looking for a target.

"You want to tell me what we're doing here, son?"

"Somebody just punched a hole in the door on my side," Cinch said. "And you're probably going to need a new set of seatcovers, too."

"Damn. I just bought this car last year." But Kohl continued to weave a side-to-side path across the desert, spewing red-brown billows that rose ten, maybe fifteen meters into the still air. As cover went, it was pretty good. Wouldn't slow a projectile down, but it was hard to shoot what you couldn't see.

If there were any more shots, they didn't hear them, and

nothing else hit the car save for a few unlucky sage plants fanned flat under the front as they sped away.

"Here it is," Kohl said, coming up from under the driver's seat of the car. They were back at his station, parked in the garage a hundred meters from the main house. A clanky air conditioner tried to keep the big Evermore plastic prefab building cool but was losing the fight. Even so, it was 20 percent cooler inside than out. The place smelled like old lube and battery acid.

Cinch looked at the small chunk of mushroomed metal the older man held out on his palm. It appeared to be a copper-jacketed, boat-tailed bullet, the nose deformed and peeled back to show the shiny lead underneath. He picked the bullet up from Kohl's palm. "Looks like a 7mm," he said. "Hunting rifle, probably."

Kohl nodded. "Yep. Lizard gun. Everybody and his sister around here has one."

Cinch tossed the bullet into the air, caught it. "Well. If we ever get the right one, we can do comparison ballistics and get a match."

Kohl grinned. "Can't be more'n twelve, fifteen thousand such rifles west of the Impossible Mountains. Good luck."

Cinch returned the grin. "Rangers enforce the law equally, understand, without prejudice, but I tend to take it personally when somebody shoots at me," he said. "I'll find who did it. Meanwhile, I suppose I should report the shooting to the local law."

"That'd be Constable Maling, and a waste of your time. He's Tuluk's man, might as well be wearing his brand right in the center of his fat forehead."

"The law is the law," Cinch said, "until I know otherwise. Where would I find the constable?"

"This time of day? Either getting stoned at Wanita's Pub or already sleeping it off in his office. Both're in Lembukota, what passes for a town around here."

"I don't recall seeing it on the shuttle trip out."

"It's the kind of place you miss if you blink at the

wrong time. Four hundred people, maybe. Come on. I'll take you."

"Might be better if I approached the constable on my own," Cinch said. "If I can borrow your car?"

Kohl shook his head. "Your funeral, son."

"Maybe not."

As he drove toward the town, away from Kohl's cattle station, Rudyard K. "Cinch" Carston grinned. Being a Stellar Ranger was many things, but it had yet to be dull. It beat ship crewing, mining, beacon monitoring and even smuggling all to hell for interesting. Here was another backrocket planet where the locals had stepped over the line; that was why he was here. If they learned nothing else, they'd learn one thing:

It was better not to mess with the Stellar Rangers.

chapter 2

Lembukota could have been a two-street town on any of half a dozen worlds Cinch had spaced to in the past thirty years. Most of the buildings were Evermore plastic, that ugly ubiquitous shade of pale blue that most resembled the skin tone of an albino who had died of oxygen starvation. Oddly enough, the smell of the Evermore in the hot sun reminded Cinch of burned circuit boards.

The prefab slabs had been slapped and glued together with permabonder, and were thus supposed to withstand any climate a human could survive in for a minimum of a hundred and fifty years without chipping, cracking or fading. The buildings he passed in the borrowed car couldn't be any older than man's time on this world, that being a mere ninety years, but they were chipped, cracked and faded.

Maybe they had bought them used.

The town was laid out in a rough cross, with the north-south line longer than the east-west road. There were some small dirt roads that looped away from the two main roads, alleys between some of the buildings, and footpaths worn into the land by humans or domestic animals. There were horses on this world, practical given the terrain and cost of importing machinery, as well as camels and bond oxen: genetically engineered work beasts that were long-lived and strong, but short-tempered and stupid. Those who could afford machines used those instead of the oxen unless they had a true love of animals. Since manufacturing of complex machineries such as robots and other high tech gear was usually the last thing a frontier world brought on-line, it was much cheaper to breed animals from natural stock. Turn the males loose with the females, feed them, let nature build your machines the old-fashioned way. They were organic, produced useful by-products, and if all else failed you could eat them. Hard to do with a robot tractor that had set you back ninety thousand MUs.

Cinch made one pass up the north–south road, circled around and slowly fanned the length of the east-west street. Here, some people had planted small trees or shrubbery; there were some flowering plants and a few gardens. The more industrious among the locals had painted their houses or storefronts in bright colors, though most of those had faded under the sun's bright hammer.

Cinch filed it all away, noting the locations of the medical building, the constable's office and town hall, the pubs and markets. A few children moved about in the noon sun, listless in the heat, and he saw a woman leave a small housing unit and hurry to a solar-powered motorcycle. The solar cells formed a small peaked roof over the trike, and the quiet electric engine drove it on hard silicone wheels. A bumpy ride on a dirt road, but faster than walking and doubtlessly cooler.

The constable's office was closed. In a chipvox that tried to sound like a sexy woman and almost did, the door-admit computer said, "Constable Maling is not in at the moment. You may leave a message, or if you have an emergency he may be reached by name code on Celcom-net. Thank you."

Cinch declined to leave a message and walked back to the GE car. What was the name of the pub Kohl had mentioned? Wanita's? That was on the lower arm of the north-south road.

The pub wasn't particularly imposing from the outside.

It bore a windowless facade, painted a once-bright maroon, now faded to a tepid and hazy rose pink. A double set of sliding polarized glass doors in gritty tracks kept most of the heat and light out. Inside the inner doors, the main room held a long, curved bar, wood or a good imitation of it, backed by alternating mirrors and holograms. A table flushtop cooler was set under the mirrors. There were fifteen or sixteen bolted-to-the-floor pedestal tables that would seat three comfortably, four less so; cast lightweight plastic chairs that wouldn't do much damage if thrown; a CD-ROMbox for music and vids parked next to a public com half-kiosk. Like ten thousand pubs on two dozen other worlds.

A tender stood behind the bar, a tall dark-skinned woman with kinky, short red hair, dressed in a loose coverall and apron. Two customers stood at the other end of the bar, eighteen or twenty more sat at the tables, drinking, smoking hazestik, or playing with other legal recreational chems: dust, spike, eyeleaf. The hazestik smoke smelled like crushed green crab apples.

Everybody in the place saw him come in.

Some of them stared openly, some of them used the mirrors, some watched but peripherally. But they all looked.

Cinch grinned. This was a small planet, populationwise, no more than a hundred thousand permanent settlers, most of them well east of the big mountain range two hundred klicks from here. He wasn't wearing any kind of uniform, just a set of lightweight hot climate dryskins—hat, shirt, pants, orthoplastic boots—and his gun rig. He had a holobadge and ranger ID tucked into his wallet, but those didn't show. He was a couple of centimeters taller than average but nothing to gape at; fairly muscular but not overly so; old enough to look grown, young enough not to creak. Nobody would cross the street to admire his handsomeness, but likely nobody would cross the street to avoid him for being ugly. Put him in a room with ten other basic male Terran stockers of mixed races and he'd fade. You know that guy in the back of the room? The one who sorta blends into the background? Well, no, that's not him, it's the guy *next* to him. . . .

Since most of the patrons here were also armed, frontiers being somewhat dangerous places, Cinch didn't particularly stand out. But he could tell they knew who he was. Small-town grapevine com was faster than a hot Salinas Drive starhopper.

Listen up, folks: There's a new ranger in town.

Cinch made as if he didn't notice the stares. He walked to the bar. Said to the tender, "What's the local beer called?"

She grinned at him, showing almost-but-not-quite-perfect teeth, which probably meant they were her own. "Hitch," she said.

"Hitch?"

"Yeah, 'cause it'll melt the hard chrome plating off a blueweed combine's trailer hitch."

He gave her a smile in return. "That'll do."

"A half liter of Hitch, coming up." She pulled a chilled ceramic mug from a cooler and filled it from a tap. Knifed the foam off the top and added more beer, set it on the counter in front of him.

He reached for his credit wafer.

"First one's on the house," she said. "I'm Wanita. This is my place."

"Cinch Carston," he said, offering his hand.

"The ranger," she said.

He nodded. Her grip was firm, her hands tough but with smooth calluses. The half-length sleeves revealed veined forearms and etched musculature. That was enough for him to know she was in good shape under that baggy coverall and apron. She stood in balance, so she knew some kind of fighting art or maybe was a dancer or gymnast.

The beer was much better than the warning. He took two swallows, savored it, then put the mug down. "Which one is the constable?"

She lost her smile. "Table in the back, far right."

Cinch glanced that way. There were two men at the table.

"Maling's the fat, stupid-looking one with the neon green cap and the wine stains on his shirt," she said. "The bodybuilder in the spandoflex tights is Anjing Lobang. He's Tuluk's chief pistoleer and headbreaker, a real sweet-meat."

He looked at her. "Doesn't sound as if you particularly like either one of them."

"If you want to shoot them both in the back right now, I'll swear it was self-defense." She grinned again.

"Thanks for the beer, Wanita."

"My pleasure, Ranger."

Cinch took a deep breath and let it escape slowly. Might as well get it over with.

He walked to the rear table, aware that Lobang avoided looking at him and the constable couldn't stop watching him. When he was two meters away he stopped. "Constable Maling?"

The fat man wiped his mouth with one hand. No veins visible there under the insulating blubber. "Yeah, that's right. Who're you?"

"I'm Carston, Stellar Rangers."

"My, my," Lobang said, his back still to Cinch. "A real, live Stellar Ranger. Well, I'm impressed."

Lobang had black hair, buzzed short, and the swelling lines of his heavy back and shoulder muscles were easily visible through the skintights. From the way he sat in the plastic chair, Cinch could see his sidearm. It looked to be an M-frame 12mm Vapen, a electroplasma fléchette pistol. It was made of wound supercarb fiber, light-weight, impervious to ordinary wear, accurate to a hundred meters, and had a built-in laser sight. The high-velocity darts it fired were designed to tumble after they hit something solid, tearing great holes as they did so. It held fifteen rounds unless an extended magazine was fitted and since the mag's base was flush to the butt, fifteen it was. Fine piece of hardware, expensive, built for use and not looks.

Cinch's own weapon, left to him by his grandfather, was a Smith & Wesson CGLS, old when his grandfather owned it. The stainless-steel semiauto used a magazine powered by a double cylinder of highly compressed and esoteric gases, a special enzyme added to keep them from liquefying. The projectiles were teflex-coated lead starfish bullets. When one of the bullets hit something the consistency of tissue or harder, they expanded from 9mm to 15mm in the shape of a starfish, even at the modest 300 meters/second subsonic velocities at which they flew. The magazine held only six shots before he had to reload.

In a long-range shootout from behind cover, against somebody with a Vapen, Cinch would be outgunned.

At two meters, it didn't make any difference at all. Either gun would kill you just as dead as the other.

"What can I do for you?" the constable said.

"There was a shooting earlier today, on Gustav Kohl's station. Somebody shot through the door of his GE car while he and I were in it."

The fat man shrugged. "Anybody hurt?"

"No."

Maling essayed a nervous smile. "Prob'ly an accident. Somebody potting at a lizard missed, you caught a stray round, ricochet, maybe. Happens now and then. Long as nobody was hurt it's nothing to worry about."

Lobang turned. His face was as muscular as the rest of him. He looked like a squirrel with nuts stuffed into his cheeks. Too many steroids, or somebody had tweaked his GH levels. His sclera were more yellow than white. His hair made a widow's peak almost reaching to his eyebrows. He was young, Cinch decided, and probably not very bright: not much blood left for the brain after feeding all that muscle mass.

Lobang said, "Yeah, them rifle bullets, they can zip a real long way when somebody misses their target." He gave Cinch an evil grin. "Got to be careful wandering around out on the plains, you do. You could get shot, eaten by a lizard, could step in a pooger hole and break your leg. This here is dangerous country, you don't know your way around it good."

Cinch restrained an urge to shake his head and laugh.

This guy must have gotten his education from kid-vids. He'd had a mustache, he probably would have twirled it.

"Funny, I don't remember saying anything about it being a rifle bullet that hit the car."

Lobang's smile faltered just a hair. Cinch could almost hear the gears turning inside the man's head as he tried to understand he'd just made a mistake.

Maling leaped in to spare Lobang: "Well, we just assumed that was what it was. Hell, even Lubbie's handcannon there won't hardly stop a real big ularsinga with one shot."

"Did I say it was only one shot?"

The constable rubbed his mouth, glanced at Lobang. The bigger man didn't turn to look at Maling, but said, "Shut up, Deter. And don't fucking call me Lubbie."

Maling nodded, a slight motion. Looked up at Cinch. "Look, Ranger, if you want to fill out a report—"

"Maybe later," Cinch cut in. "I just wanted to check in and let you know I was around. I'll be here awhile."

"Doing what? I mean, I'm the Constable—"

"—and I wouldn't think of interfering in your business," Cinch cut in again. "See you around."

What was left unsaid was: And don't you get into Stellar Ranger business. Cinch was pretty sure that Gustav Kohl's assessment of Deter Maling as bought and paid for by the local cattle baron was probably accurate. Crooked cops irritated Cinch, but it was good at least to know the local law was that way. If that was the case, Maling was already up to his butt in this business. That happened sometimes. You could deal with it.

Cinch walked to the door, using the mirrors to keep watch on Lobang. He hoped the man wasn't so stupid as to try to shoot him in the back.

Cinch nodded at Wanita as he left and achieved the sliding doors without a problem. Maybe Lobang was smarter than he looked. Too bad. Stupid crooks were so much easier to deal with.

He climbed into the car and headed back toward Kohl's

station. He needed to meet another major player, but he expected that Manis Tuluk would find a way to pay a call on him fairly soon. On a frontier world, when the rangers showed up, even rich men took notice.

chapter 3

The richest man on Roget, Manis Tuluk, was not pleased.

He sat behind his hand-carved shinestone desk, the pearly material glowing softly under the indirect lighting, and glared at Lobang. The handmade whispersilk suit he wore, which normally felt so sensual against his skin, did not comfort him. Did he have to do everything himself?

"But I thought—" Lobang began.

"No, you *didn't* think," Tuluk cut him off. "I don't pay you for your brains. If I gave you what those were worth, you couldn't afford to feed a piss ant with its jaw wired shut!" His anger made him sweat a little, and that triggered his body perfume. The scent of ripe peaches rose from Tuluk's armpits.

Lobang, for all his testosterone augmentation and muscle mass, was basically a bully. If you had a bigger stick, he would back down. The larger man stared at his boot tops.

Tuluk was too rich and too old to have to put up with this kind of shit but he *had* mellowed somewhat. Thirty years ago, he would have pulled his tangler from the desk and fried Lobang's brains for such a stupid stunt. Of course, even at this range, he might have missed, given the

16

tiny size of the target. Then again, good help was always hard to find, and it was a small planet. Lobang did have his uses. He had to remember to think of Lobang as a favorite dog. Sometimes it was going to pee on the rug and that was all there was to it.

"I'll explain it to you. When you shot at the ranger, what would have happened, do you *think,* if you had hit him?"

"He'd be dead," Lobang said, smiling because he had what he was sure was the right answer.

Tuluk nodded. "That's right. He'd be dead. And they'd feed him to the recyclers or the furnaces and that would be that, right?"

"Right. End of problem."

"No, stupid, that would *not* be the 'end of problem!' If we kill this ranger in such a way that any moron with an IQ equal to his boot size can *see* it is murder, then the next star hopper will bring more rangers than fleas on a field cat! Rangers take care of their own. They would turn over every rock on the planet to find the killer and in the process would find out a whole lot of things I would not want them to find out!"

Mercifully, Lobang did not say anything.

"I will make it simple," Tuluk said. "Yes, we want the ranger to either go away or get dead. But if he dies, it has to look like an accident."

The dim bulb that was Lobang's mind glowed to life. Six, maybe eight watts. "Ah. I get it."

Jesus. The man could almost pick himself up with one hand, but he had the reasoning ability of a tree stump. Nice puppy. Now, you scratch at the door if you want to go out, you hear? Hell, might as well send him to take care of his biomechanical kin.

"All right. Go and see to the springdog. I want it ready to use, but I want it kept out of sight until I tell you. And nobody looks crooked at the ranger unless I say so."

"Yes, M. Tuluk."

After Lobang left, Tuluk leaned back and steepled his

fingers, thinking about the problem. He should have killed Gus Kohl fifty years ago, when they'd still been friends and he could have gotten away with it. Now the old bastard was dug in, had enough money so he didn't need to sell and was too stubborn to be scared off. He was a major impediment in Tuluk's plans, and now he had this damned ranger nosing around. Not good. Not good at *all*.

Tuluk shook his head. He'd maybe made a mistake, trying to scare Gus away. He should have known better. But it was done now, and he had to live with the consequences. If he could keep things quiet so the ranger came up empty, that would solve part of the problem. If the man filed a report and left, Tuluk would be more careful next time. But if the ranger got too close to something he shouldn't—and God knew there was enough of that—then the ranger would have to be dealt with, one way or another. There was too much at stake to let anybody get in the way now.

Tuluk had his spies in place; he would keep a close watch on the situation and see how it developed. Rangers weren't supermen, after all, they put their pants on one leg at a time like everybody else. Maybe he would poke around and then go away. Even though Lobang had tried to kill him, maybe he would buy the accident scenario.

Yeah, right. And maybe Tuluk would learn how to walk on water, too.

He spoke into the servant call on his desk. "Lipas, bring me a whisky."

A minute later the butler arrived, bearing a glass containing precisely fifty-eight cc's of the best single-malt scotch in the galaxy, chilled, two cubes of ice. A bottle of the made-on-Terra liquor cost enough to support a middle-class family here on Roget comfortably for six months; Tuluk had a case of it in his wine cellar. He allowed himself two glasses a day, though usually not this early in the afternoon.

He sipped the whisky, enjoyed the smoky taste as it

flowed smoothly down his throat. Then he sighed. Why was his life so much harder than everybody else's? There were always so many problems. It wasn't fair.

He sipped the whisky. No, it definitely wasn't fair.

chapter 4

Cinch had accepted Kohl's offer of a place to stay. He had plenty of room, he said, and Tuluk owned the only hotel in town, a situation that might make security somewhat frail. Even rangers had to sleep sometime.

The verdict wasn't in on M. Tuluk yet, but since Kohl was the citizen most responsible for Cinch being here, he tended to trust him. He liked the older man, and unless he came across something that said otherwise, assumed he was probably a more or less upright citizen. A person didn't have to be pure white to be a good guy. Cinch himself had done his share of things illegal, and sometimes the ranger methods might seem to stretch the boundries of the law a bit. The way Cinch looked at it, the intent was more important than a technicality. On a civilized world, with established rules and regs, there were recourses to handle nearly every little thing. On a frontier world, sometimes minor points had to be overlooked in the interest of greater justice. Somebody had to decide in those cases, and often enough it was the ranger whose butt was on the line.

He'd put Kohl in that category. He *could* be a crook, of course, but even stupid crooks seldom called the rangers in to investigate themselves.

The room Kohl gave him was large, lit by filtered skylights, had the usual bedroom furniture and a small fresher attached with a toilet and shower. Cinch had stayed in worse places.

He unpacked his gear. Took a few minutes to assemble his plasma rifle. It was more like a carbine, the barrel only a little over forty centimeters long, but accurate and hard-hitting out to seven or eight hundred meters once he got it sighted in. He'd have to do that soon. If a handgun like the one Tuluk's pistoleer carried would barely stop the local carnivores, Cinch needed to be carrying something bigger than his Smith if he did any outback work. And if somebody started shooting at him from long range, he wanted something he could hit back with. An expended uranium slug traveling at over a thousand meters a second would make a hole in just about anything short of full battle armor.

The scan on the bone he collected confirmed his guess about the metal molecules. Somebody had sicced a biomech on the dead bull, probably a springdog, maybe a chopper, unless the local lizards had somebody doing some fairly complex dentistry on them. Cinch grinned at the idea of a frontier dentist capping the teeth of a wild reptile that could take an arm off with one bite.

Biomechs wouldn't be all that common on a world this far out from the main stellar groups. The technology to build them didn't exist here yet; that meant they were imported and only somebody with a hefty credit account could afford to own and keep one repaired and running properly. That didn't mean it was Tuluk—he wasn't the only rich man on the planet—but it did point in his general direction. There were ways to trace such things, even when somebody tried to hide them. He would begin that process.

He printed out the results of the bonescan, put the sample into an evidence tube and sealed the mechanism with the date and time and his personal code. He would forward it to the ranger vaults when he had a chance. He would also uplink a verbal report into the comnet. In theory, the pulse would be beamed to the nearest transmission center and downloaded into a fast mailship. Given the time it took to get there and then get carried to within spitting dis-

tance of Regional Ranger HQ—radio still being lightslow
and tachyon transmission an iffy thing on its best day—
Cinch couldn't expect any useful advice or help for days,
weeks or maybe even months. As usual, the old maxim of
"One planet, one ranger" held true.

He went into the fresher, used the facilities, took a quick
shower, dressed in clean clothes. Might as well go and see
what else he could learn from Kohl.

Gustav Kohl had taste, Cinch gave him that. The room
he'd designated as the library had been paneled in some
dark local wood, polished to a dull sheen. Shelves of hard-
copy books, tapes, and infoballs lined the walls. There
were two computer consoles, a holoset, and four comfortable stuffed chairs covered in leather, probably from his
own cattle, Cinch guessed. Some nice, if not spectacular,
artwork on the walls, plus a small statue of Saint Dirisha,
the patron of close combat, on one of the shelves. The
statuette was of a slim and muscular woman staring off
into the distance at some unseen enemy; she was portrayed
naked and unarmed, save for her own trained hands and
feet. According to the mythology, these hands and feet had
been sufficient in themselves to defeat a small army. Most
rangers liked Dirisha and considered her their personal
saint. The place had a nice odor, a blend of leather and
furniture polish.

"Something to drink or smoke?" Kohl offered.

"I'm fine. Couple of questions I would like to ask."

"Ask, son. What I know, you can have. I didn't call the
rangers because I was bored."

Before Cinch could speak, however, the big wooden
library door slid open and a vision of beauty danced
in.

"Grampa, I need to go into—oh, hello."

She was short, petite, with dark hair cut in a short and
feathery cap that framed an almost elfin face. Her eyes
were electric blue, her smile warm and wide, and she
wore a gauzy green caftanlike garment over skintights
that revealed as much as they hid. She was quite lovely,
strikingly so, and carried herself with that look of invul-

nerability only the young can bring off successfully. Her perfume was faint, something musky. Cinch guessed that she was eighteen or nineteen standards. If he had been thirty years younger, hell, even twenty years younger, he would have walked through a forest of brambles bare-assed just to have a woman like her smile at him that way.

Youth was surely wasted on the young.

Kohl shook his head, a man put-upon. "Closed doors don't mean much to some people around here," he said to Cinch. "Best you keep yours locked if you don't want company. This is Baji Kohl, my great-granddaughter. Baji, this is Ranger Carston."

She batted her lashes at him. "Should I call you 'Ranger' or 'Mr. Carston'?"

"Cinch will do. Very nice to meet you, Ms. Kohl."

"Call me Baji."

Cinch nodded at her.

"Baji's father, my good-for-little grandson, Anaki, is offworld negotiating the blueweed contract for next season. He gets away from Roget every chance he gets."

"Nice to meet you, too, Cinch. Grampa, I need to go to Madeline's to pick up my new boots. Paku won't let me take the car unless you tell him it's okay."

"Baji, my little tumbleweed, do you think I invited the Stellar Ranger here to pass the time of day? I don't want you on the road alone until we get this mess cleared up—"

"I won't *be* alone, Gramp, I'm taking Hadji, he'll chew the leg off anybody who gets too close. I have my gun. And I promise I'll be back before dark."

Kohl shook his head. "I would rather you didn't—"

"Please, Gramp, please . . . ?"

The older man sighed. "All right. But I want you checked in before 1800—"

She ran to him, bent, and kissed him on the top of the head. "Thanks, Gramp. I'll be careful."

"If you see any sign of the raj I want you on the god-damn com calling here, you hear me?"

"The raj won't bother me," she said. "You know that."

"Do what I say or you stay here."

"All right. But you're wrong about them."

She turned and left, giving Cinch a brief smile as she departed. He thought he saw something in the expression, a hint of interest. Right. Wishful thinking on his part.

After she was gone, Kohl shook his head. "Got me twisted around her little finger," he said. "She's a good kid but I do spoil her. You had some questions?"

Cinch nodded. More now than before. He decided to follow up on the newest one first.

"What is the raj?"

Kohl returned the nod. "Pick up stuff fast, don't you? Raj—that's short for 'djalan raja'—means loosely 'the highwaymen.' A local group of banditos. They hide out in the foothills to the northeast. Not talking big time here, they're petty crooks, they sneak into outbuildings and swipe stuff they can use or sell. Kids, mostly, led by a couple of malcontents. Only good thing about them is that they hit Tuluk more than anybody else. Course, that's the rule for thieves, isn't it? Go where the money is. Anyway, the head bandito is a young man named Pandjang Meritja. He used to work for Tuluk, there was some unpleasantness there, and Tuluk had him horsewhipped in front of half the town. The boy didn't take it well, but he was smart enough to know he couldn't go up against Tuluk in the open. So he hits him in the credit wafer. Smart, but he could steal ten times as much as he does every day for the next hundred years and not make a dent in Tuluk's interest income."

"But you're still worried about your granddaughter's safety?"

He shook his head. "No, not really. Pan wouldn't lay a finger on her. First thing is, he knows I'd hunt him down and deball him with a dull shovel if he did. Second thing is, I do believe he worships the ground she walks on. He'd jump off a cliff into a spearshrub patch before he'd do anything to even make her frown. I just don't want her associating with them. Sooner or later Tuluk is going to get tired of being harassed and turn his goons loose to take care of the raj. I don't want Baji in the way.

"No, what I worry about is what killed my bull and who sent it. If something happened to Baji, whoever did it would be dead before the next sun went down—but that wouldn't be much comfort."

If he expected a lecture on the law, he wasn't going to get it. Cinch would do the same thing. "Okay."

"One other thing I ought to mention. You met a relative of Pan's when you went into town. His sister. She owns the best pub in Lembukota."

"Wanita's his sister?"

"The same."

Ah. That maybe explained part of her reaction to Tuluk's local law and hired gun.

Good to know.

There wasn't an awful lot more he got from Kohl. He had been beset by a whole lot of minor annoyances in the last year—animals killed, water holes soured, com towers cut down, power stations shorted out. He couldn't prove it, but he was certain Tuluk was behind it. The man had offered to buy him out, and Kohl had refused. Almost immediately afterward, unlucky things had started to happen.

"You reported it to the constable?"

Kohl laughed, almost a cackle. He was truly amused. "Hell, son, I might as well have written my complaints on a rock and pitched it down a sinkhole for all the good that would do. If Constable Maling saw Tuluk's herdsmen marching down the main street of town carrying the heads of my whole herd stuck on top of sharp sticks, he would allow as how the cows must have died of heart attacks and the boys were just having a little fun."

Cinch nodded. It was, after all, one of the main reasons anybody ever called the Stellar Rangers on these worlds. When you couldn't get satisfaction from the local law, you looked elsewhere. Mostly the frontier types just loaded their guns and took care of it themselves. A man or woman stomped on your toes, why, you just smiled and cut them off at the knees. Unless you were outnumbered in a major way, as seemed to be the case here.

"Well. We'll see if we can't get to the bottom of this," Cinch said.

Kohl nodded. "I appreciate it."

There were a lot of things he could do, and Cinch would begin doing them. Meanwhile, his experience had taught him that just being here was enough to stir the pot some. He'd see what happened when things began to settle out of the brew.

chapter 5

Like many frontier world people with a lot of real estate, Kohl had a shooting range on his property. The station's range was of the most basic kind—no holographic targets or scoring computers, no automatic setters or turners. Here, the range consisted of an eight-meter-high berm of catdozed dirt, packed tight into a U-shape, with two hundred meters of bare ground in front of it. A shooter could set up whatever crude targets were available in front of the earthen backstop and have at them, without worrying that stray rounds would go far.

As Cinch looked at the range, he smiled. Even if the misses or richochets did escape the berms, there wasn't anything to the sides or behind them for as far as he could see apt to be damaged anyhow. The house and outbuildings were all five hundred meters in the opposite direction.

There was a skeletal structure at the end of the range, basically an Evermore roof on posts that provided blue-tinted shade, with a shooting bench and a couple of rests for rifles under it. Three or four stools, a few plastic stands with self-healing flat bull's-eye targets, and a beat-up solar-powered electric open-topped cart full of pepper poppers completed the equipment available. The poppers, flat steel plates roughly man-sized, looked in silhouette much like an upright and erect dick stuck through a ball. They had timed spring motors on their bases. You set them up, backed off and shot at them. If you missed, well, you missed. If you hit one, it fell down. After a few seconds, it would stand up again under the impetus of the small motor. The big advantage to shooting such targets aside from their simple reactiveness was the satisfying *clang* they made when you connected with them. Instant feedback.

Cinch put his rifle and shooting bag on the bench and went to set his targets. Even though the sun had just come up, it was already hot. For some reason nobody had yet explained satisfactorily, most of the E-type worlds man had discovered, the ones with the right gravity, air and water for more or less unaided human survival, were either tropical or desert over a great deal of their surface. Sure, there were some ice planets, and a few that were temperate with large oceans, but they were in the minority. The one advantage of the desert was the low humidity. At least the sweat evaporated instead of puddling in your boots.

He set one bull's-eye and one pepper popper at two hundred meters, just in front of the berm. A second like pair he put at one hundred meters. He put up three poppers each at fifty and twenty-five meters and the last two steel targets at seven meters. Most actual combat shooting in police or civilian matters took place at seven meters or less. The old ranger saying, taken from some long-lost Terran police agency, was "Three shots, three feet, three seconds." A foot was, Cinch supposed, a measurement based on the human foot of the same name, about a third of a meter, and very close for gunplay.

He returned to the bench, put his plasma rifle on it, and checked the powerpak and dot-scope settings. He switched the scope on. A tiny holographic red dot the size of a pinhead floated in the air a couple centimeters above the receiver. You put the dot over the target and, in theory, the rifle would drive the bullet right there, corrected for parallax and dead center at two hundred meters. Farther than that, you either adjusted the sight or held high, close range, you held low. Of course, every time you broke the weapon down for transport, it jiggled the setting. Wasn't supposed to, according to the manufacturer, but it did. It didn't make much difference, maybe a fingernail's width at twenty-five meters, a handspan or more at three hundred meters. Thing was, at long range, a few centimeters either way could get you in real trouble if somebody was shooting back at you.

Cinch pulled his spotting scope from his bag and set it on the bench, dialed in two hundred meters, and focused it on the bull's-eye target. He loaded a plate of slugs into the rifle, adjusted the step-up transformer and capacitor, clicked the safety off. He put his earplugs in to block the sound. The rifle mostly made a flamethrower's whoosh that wasn't too bad, but the slug broke the sound barrier before it got far and that *crack* was fairly loud. He pulled a stool up and laid the rifle's barrel into one of the rests. He put the dot on the target, took a couple of breaths then held the third one. He concentrated on his heartbeat, waited for the brief interlude between the lubb and the dupp, and squeezed the trigger—

The muzzle blast of the rifle was fierce as superheated plasma spewed forth. The recoil, though dampened by the biogel pad in the stock's butt, was also fairly potent.

Come the sound barrier being cracked open, a hard slap at his protected ears.

When he'd recovered, he flicked the safety on, put the rifle down, and looked through the scope.

High and right, he saw. Five centimeters up, eight to the right. He could almost hear his grandfather tsking. *What's the matter son, you gone blind?* He smiled at the memory. He used the punch-pick sight tool to unlock the sight, then adjusted it for elevation and windage.

The second shot was even with the bull's-eye but still a hair to the right. *Damn boy, my mother shoots better than that, and she's dead.*

He made another adjustment.

The third shot was centered in the black of the bull's-eye, maybe a couple millimeters low, but that could be him and not the gun. Close enough, Grandpa? *For government work, son, but not much else.* Cinch grinned and locked the sight settings.

He unloaded the weapon, shut the power off, sprayed

cleaner through the barrel and action, then ran an absorbent patch down the bore to remove any fouling. The rifle was zeroed and there wasn't any need to play with it anymore. Anybody could shoot a rifle. Hell, with the settings locked in, his great-grandmother *could* drive tacks with the thing at this range.

The handgun was another matter. Sidearms were, generally speaking, underpowered and inaccurate past short range. Then again, they were what you were likely to have when the shit went down, and it was a good idea to be as adept with them as you could.

Cinch's gun rode in a vat-grown horsehide holster with a pinchnose that held it firmly in place. He ought to look into getting a new holster while he was here, there being horses around. The pinchnose allowed him to carry without a safety strap, so the gun could be snatched from the holster at speed limited only by his reaction and skill. The trigger guard and trigger were covered, so he wasn't apt to shoot himself in the ass if he fumbled on the draw.

Cinch stepped away from the bench and faced the closest pepper poppers. He whipped his hand down, drew the pistol smoothly, and brought it up, catching his right hand in his left in a two-handed grip, feet planted firmly in an isosceles stance. Moving from left to right, he fired double taps, two shots at each target, aiming for the heart. Even through the sound-deadening plugs he heard the steel ring as the four bullets hit. *Ting-ting! Ting-ting!*

The two poppers fell over slowly, like a pair of simultaneously chainsawed trees toppling.

While he waited for them to reset, he fired the last two rounds in his pistol at the twenty-five-meter poppers, taking more time to aim and squeeze off the shots. *Tink! Tink!*

He reloaded and went through a series of drills, double and triple taps at close range, slow fire at the longer distances. He was able to keep about half his shots on the metal at a hundred meters, a third of them at two hundred. Of course the bullets didn't have much zing when they got that far and the poppers rang but did not fall under the impact.

He wasn't the best or the fastest ranger with a handgun;

there were younger officers who could outdraw and out-shoot him easily in a qualifying drill, but he practiced enough to feel comfortable with his ability. And since he had been in more than a few real life-or-death gun duels, he had that advantage over some of the hotter players. Shooting at a target that shot back was altogether different than plinking on the range against a clock.

She probably thought she was sneaking up on him but Cinch noticed Baji walking toward the range while she was still a couple of minutes away. He pretended not to see her, continuing his drills.

She arrived. "Pretty good shooting," she said as he hol-stered his pistol.

He turned and smiled at her. She wore red skintights and a flared cap, molded boot slippers that reached half-way up her calves. Very attractive and she knew it.

"I get by," he said.

"I'm not much good with one of those," she said, gesturing at the pistol. "I can shoot a rifle okay. My grandfather taught me. We used to go lizard hunting when I was young."

Cinch smiled. When she was young.

"Can I try it?"

"Sure."

He showed her how the weapon worked, told her where to hold if she used the mechanical sights, and that the dot worked just like her rifle if she preferred that.

"Why wouldn't you use the dot? Isn't it faster and more accurate than the notch thing?"

"Yes. But if the power fails and you don't know how to use the mechanicals, it could be a problem. At very close range, a meter or two, you don't need either, you just point it like you would your finger and shoot."

"I see. Very clever." She treated him to one of her smiles. Took a deep breath and pushed her chest at him.

It wasn't much, nothing too obvious, but he smiled again. God, this little girl was flirting with him. He was al-most old enough to be her grandfather and she was letting him know she was interested in him that way.

Cinch had to admit to himself that it didn't hurt his ego

any. Then again, he wasn't about to screw around with the great-granddaughter of the only man on this planet he could trust, aside from the fact he preferred women with a lot more life experience than this child. Pretty, yes. Sexually attractive, sure, and old enough to be legal, but not for Cinch. What would they talk about afterward? Or before, for that?

She shot well enough, managed to hit the nearest targets okay, but missed at the longer ranges. She also kept putting herself within reach:

"Maybe if you stood behind me and helped me hold it right?"

It was all Cinch could do to keep from laughing. She probably thought she was being so clever. When he stood behind her and steadied her hands with his own, she allowed the pistol's slight recoil to shove her back against him. The musk perfume was stronger with his nose almost in her hair. Her buttocks under her skintights were firm against his thighs, and he was tempted to push against her—for about two seconds. Instead, he stepped back a little and said, "Good shot."

He'd gotten past the point in his life where he let his little head do the thinking for him. It had, he had to admit, taken some years to manage that. If he'd been twenty-five, hell, even forty, he'd have her on her back on the bench by now, devil take anybody passing by. But not these days.

"I think that's enough for now," he said.

Baji frowned, an expression that vanished quickly.

He showed her how to field-strip the pistol and clean it. She did not care in the least, but she pretended to be fascinated as she watched him. She kept trying. The double entendres began getting less subtle.

"My, that rod surely does fit tightly when you put it in the barrel, doesn't it?"

"Yes, it does."

"That why you put that lubricant in first, so it will go in easier?"

"More to ream it out and leave it clean, actually."

He could play. It might not be too smart, but it made him grin. Talk was not action.

She was getting frustrated and he didn't want to hurt her feelings, so he decided to give her something. "Listen," he said, "I have to go into town. Maybe we can have lunch when I get back, if you're not too busy?"

Her face lit up, she smiled, then quickly tried to cover it with a pretended indifference. "Oh, sure, if I'm around when you get back."

He would bet his pension she'd be around when he got back, but he merely nodded.

"What are you going to do in town, if it's okay to ask?"

"Oh, this and that. I thought I might talk to a couple of people, ask a few questions. Boring background stuff."

"Would Wanita Meritja be one of the people?"

He shrugged. "Could be."

"You want to be careful around her."

"Oh? Why is that?"

She glanced at the ground. "Well, her brother, you know, he's the leader of the raj. You might not want to get too close to her, she tells him stuff. Plus her reputation and all."

"Reputation?"

She found something fascinating under the roof of the range building and stared at it. "Oh, it's nothing, really. I probably shouldn't have mentioned it. Never mind."

"Okay." He was willing to let it drop.

"It's just that, well, you know, she is considered, ah, somewhat ... loose."

Now he did chuckle. Loose? He hadn't heard that term in a long time. For some reason he did not understand, frontier-world morality was very often straitlaced. On civilized planets, sexual mores were up to the players. Very little was considered immoral, less was illegal, between consenting adults. There were laws protecting children and against deadly violence, of course, but what you did in private—or sometimes publicly—was pretty much your own business. Cinch had been in communes of two hundred people where everybody had engaged in sex with everybody else, sometimes by the busload at once, and nobody thought anything of it. On some of the outplanets, if a man or woman had more than one lover or they weren't legally contracted, they were considered wanton sluts. Amazing.

What she thought of his amusement Cinch didn't know, but she appeared to be angered by it. "Don't get me wrong, I *like* Wanita, but there are some in town who call her 'lidah mulut.' "

Cinch raised an eyebrow. Must have missed that term in his language lessons.

"It means 'magic mouth,' " she said. She blushed as she spoke.

Cinch's grin was altogether too wide to be polite. Well, well. Now *that* was interesting news. Wanita was, as far as he could tell, an adult.

"I'll be very careful," he said, still smiling.

She wasn't dull, just inexperienced. "You're laughing at me," she said.

"I'm a grown man," he said. "A trained and experienced ranger. I can take care of myself."

"I bet," she said, still miffed.

Which was pretty much the end of that conversation.

chapter 6

Before he left for town Cinch stopped to speak to Kohl.
The older man was in his office, scanning computer data
on a holoprojection. He looked up at Cinch through the
ghostly, transluscent heads-up display.

"Okay if I borrow your car again?"

"Go ahead. You clear this up, you can have the car and
five more like it. No bribe intended."

"None accepted."

Kohl chewed on his lip and looked thoughtful. He cycled the computer off-line and leaned back, but did not
speak.

"Something?"

The older man nodded. "Yeah. I don't know quite how
to put this, son. Baji is, well, *taken* with you."

"She seems to be a good kid."

"Uh huh, that she is. And legally a grown woman, too,
so it ain't my bidness how she chooses to spend most of
her time, outside of I feel responsible for her personal
safety and all. I don't choose her friends, she don't pay
much attention to my warnings about who she should run
with anyhow. She danced past here a minute ago like she
was going out on her first date."

He paused, as if trying to figure a way to say something. The beginnings of a frown formed.

Cinch saw where Kohl was going. "If I'd started a fam-

ily when I was her age, your great-grandfather would be
just about old enough to be *my* granddaughter, M. Kohl.
She might be of *legal* age but we both know she's still not
much more than a baby."

Kohl's expression cleared. "Thanks, son. I appreciate
that. I know I'm just a meddling old fart, but I surely don't
want anything bad to happen to her. No matter how good
you might be in the short run, you'd be moving on soon
and it would break her heart."

"I'll tell her she reminds me of my sister," Cinch said.

"She'll hate that. But thanks again."

"No problem, M. Kohl."

"Call me Gus, son."

The two men nodded at each other.

As Cinch walked through the dusty heat and cooked-dirt
smell toward the garage, he nodded to himself. That
wasn't so bad. If Baji had been thirty or forty, it might
have been different. He could have ignored Gus's thinly
veiled warning and felt perfectly comfortable about it.
There was nothing wrong with his sex drive and it had
been awhile since he'd taken it out for a spin. But Baji
was just a child, her hormones and body notwithstanding.
If she'd grown up in, say, the commune on Altius, she'd
have been to bed with a whole lot more lovers than Cinch
by her age, and maybe he'd have thought about it even as
young as she was. But here? The old man hadn't needed
to say anything and Cinch's noble capitulation didn't hurt
him. A big part of rangering consisted of making good local connections, and he was pretty sure he had one in
Gustav Kohl now. And cradle-robbing wasn't his style.

There was work to be done, though, and he couldn't
spend too much time patting himself on the back just yet.

Lobang waved a powerful hand at the entrance reader to
Tukul's office and the chime sounded.

Tukul had already seen the man. "What?"

"The ranger, he's heading into town. In one of Kohl's
cars."

"Go get the limo. I'll be out in a minute."

Lobang turned and thudded his way down the hall. Tuluk shook his head. Lobang was supposed to be an expert in *tindju,* a fighting art that stressed balance and power. You'd think he could walk a little quieter.

Tuluk stood. He was a tall man, his skin kept pale by strict use of sunblock spray, his frame still as thin as he'd been forty years ago. He didn't exercise much but his metabolic rate was naturally high and when it began to drop a bit a few years back, he'd had it augmented with hypothalmic implants. He didn't want to sweat over it, but it was a point of personal pride that he was not fat.

He pulled his tangler from the desk and slipped the device into his pants pocket. The weapon was small, a long and narrow rectangle of smooth black aluminum two fingers wide by fifteen or sixteen centimeters long, a double-button firing stud on the opposite sides. Tanglers were short-range weapons. Outside of ten meters you might as well throw one as use it, and the narrow beam it spat meant you had to aim at the target or miss. Inside its range and more or less lined up, the tangler would scramble the neurons in a complex brain enough so the resulting short circuit would fry the organ pretty much beyond repair, save by a neurosurgeon with a hot hand and a full bank of regen gear backing him. Unless the target wore a faraday-net, the tangler was as deadly a close-range weapon as you would need. It was quiet, held three charges, and was as illegal as hell, even on this planet. It always smelled like baked walnuts when you fired it.

Tuluk didn't like guns, even air guns. They were too noisy and bulky, and the mark of somebody without finesse. A tangler was more subtle. It showed class. He didn't expect to use it; that's what he had dogmuscle like Lobang for, but one never knew. A careful man always kept as many options open as possible regarding his personal safety.

He moved toward the house's entrance. Even though he planned to keep things quiet when it came to the ranger, he needed to see the man and get a feel for who he was. Too many assumptions usually came up with at least one bad one and he hadn't gotten where he was by being wrong that often.

There was a big man in freight handlers's coveralls sitting in the corner mumbling to himself when Cinch ambled into Wanita's pub. The ranger noted a few faces he had seen the time before, a few new ones he didn't recognize. He walked to the bar where the black woman met him and flashed her slightly imperfect smile. "Cinch," she said. "What can I get you?"

"Hitch will do it." He tendered his credit wafer. Wanita took it, ran it over the scanner, passed it back.

He sipped the beer. The sharp taste with a hint of bitterness tickled his mouth. There was a faint scent of yeast in the beer.

"Getting any work done?"

He looked at Wanita. "Some. You hear anything from your brother lately?"

She shrugged. "He calls now and then. He's not part of your problem."

"Didn't say he was. I just like to know who the players are when I join a new game. I might want to have a word with him if he's available."

"He might not be disposed to get too close to a stellar ranger, given his situation."

"Could be a peace-seal meeting. He walks after it's over."

"I'll see what I can do."

The man in the corner mumbled a little louder, talking to himself or some unseen companion in a tight, angry voice.

"That's Muatan," Wanita said. "Goes by 'Mutt.' He loads cargo at the mag-lev trainyard. His battery charge is always a little low, if you know what I mean."

Cinch looked at the big man.

She answered his unasked question. "Mutt doesn't like medics. So he treats himself with his own combination of chem. Bourbon and sloweed, mostly, a little hup for balance. When he gets the proportions right, he's harmless."

"And when he gets the proportions wrong?"

"He usually puts four or five people in the mediplex for a week-long overhaul and spends the next month or two in the constable's lockup for assault."

Cinch nodded, sipped at his beer. Frontier worlds attracted a lot of loose nuts and bolts. "Mind your own business, I'll mind mine" was a strong ethic on most outback planets. If you knew somebody was a mean drunk or a slip-psych, you stayed out of their way.

The sliding door grated open and Lobang stepped inside, followed by a slightly smaller version of himself. A third man entered, tall, pale, older, dressed in expensive green silks and custom orthocast boots. Despite the heat that wafted in through the closing door, the man looked cool and in control. A faint smell of body cologne rode the warm air, something like peaches.

Cinch didn't need to be told who the tall man was.

Like bodyguards for a planetary president, Lobang and the other man moved into the room, searching for danger. They walked to a table with the tall man bracketed between them. The tall man sat. Lobang and his partner remained standing. Lobang kept his hand thumb-hooked in his belt, near his pistol butt.

"That's—" Wanita began.

"—Tuluk," Cinch finished.

"You've met?"

"Not yet." He sipped his beer and turned most of his attention on Wanita. He could see the newly arrived trio easily enough in the mirror behind the black woman.

"Brilly—that's the other thug—he'll be coming to get Tuluk's drink in a second," she said. "Single-malt scotch. I always keep a couple of bottles for him in the cooler, his personal stock."

"Can't make much of a profit that way, can you?"

"He pays a corkage fee. As much as if I sold him some of my own cheap stuff."

Brilly moved toward the bar. Wanita pulled a whiskey glass from the bin, added two ice cubes, and had begun pouring the liquor by the time the bodyguard arrived. Cinch caught the smoky scent of the liquid as it splashed over the ice. The tender put a napkin under the glass and pushed it toward Brilly. He didn't smile or nod or otherwise acknowledge her, save to pick up the glass and napkin and return to the table where Tuluk sat waiting. He put the glass down carefully. Tuluk didn't look at it.

"—damn toejam sucker!" Mutt's voice climbed up a couple of notches and burned with anger.

Lobang flicked a glance at Mutt, then looked back at the ranger.

"Mutt gave Lobang all he could handle once," Wanita said. She wiped at the bar's top with a rag. "Shook the whole building when they slammed into the walls. Lobang beat him, but just barely. There hadn't been a whole room full of witnesses, I expect Lobang would have shot him— Mutt broke Lobang's nose and knocked out a couple of expensive teeth implants he had to have replaced."

"Interesting."

"It's the only time anybody hereabouts held their own with Lobang. He's faster than a spit-spider and those muscles aren't just for show. And he knows some fighting dances, he can break bricks and stuff with his hands."

Cinch smiled.

"Something funny?"

"That'd come in handy if a building sneaks up and tries to fall on him."

She chuckled.

Mutt stood suddenly and slapped his chair away. The lightweight plastic flew halfway across the room and bounced from a table where two women and two men were playing stack coin for demicreds. The chair knocked the small coin blocks every which way and upended four drinks.

"Jesus, Mutt! What the hell is the matter with you?" A short man stood and wiped at his lap where his drink had drenched him.

Wanita reached under the bar.

Cinch raised an eyebrow.

"Buzcom to Maling's office," she said. "If he's there, he'll come running with his trank gun in, oh, thirty or forty minutes. If we're lucky."

Mutt turned to face the small man who'd spoken. Mutt

smiled. It was not a happy expression. He started toward the smaller man.

Cinch saw the crazed look on Mutt's face and shook his head. It was a local problem, it wasn't his business; still, he was a ranger and he hated to see an innocent man get his ass kicked. Besides, he might as well let Lobang and his boss know what they were dealing with. Time to flash the flash.

"Hey," Cinch said. His voice wasn't loud, but it carried well enough for Mutt to hear. The big man turned his unblinking stare on the ranger.

"You don't want to hurt anybody," Cinch said.

"I believe I do," Mutt said. His voice belonged to a much smaller person. It was high, delicate, almost feminine. "I believe I want to smash some toejam sucker's head against the wall. Really. That's what I believe."

Cinch stepped away from the wall. "I don't think you ought to do that."

Mutt's grin grew even wider. "I believe it might be your head. How would you like that?"

"I wouldn't much like it," Cinch admitted. "Then again, I don't much think it's going to happen, either."

"Yeah, that's right, you got a gun."

"It stays in the holster."

Mutt nodded. "Call on your god, pal." He moved for Cinch.

Cinch stood still until the big man got within two meters. Mutt was big and Mutt was strong and he reached for Cinch with hands spread wide to grab. . . .

It is relatively easy to best somebody in hand-to-hand combat if you are well trained and practiced and you see them coming. A single punch or kick delivered properly will kill or maim an attacker, ending the fight almost instantly. What is harder to do, what is much riskier, is to control somebody without really damaging them. Cinch had studied fighting styles for years before he ever considered becoming a Stellar Ranger. He had been fortunate enough to happen across a legitimate Master of an ancient martial art seldom seen any more in the galaxy. It was called *denku-te*—the name meant "lightning hands"—and as practiced by an expert the style offered a player a great deal of personal protection. Perhaps only a *sumito* dancer familiar with the entire pattern of the Ninety-Seven Steps could defeat a *denku-te* expert of equal rank in a one-on-one.

Cinch was no expert, not in the same class as Master Sissu or even Marie Lu, Sissu's top student, but he knew a few moves.

Cinch stepped under the grasping hands and stole Mutt's breath with a twin-knuckle strike to his solar plexus.

Mutt grunted, now unable to breathe.

The ranger stepped to one side and jerked Mutt backward and down with a hair lock. Even as Mutt fell, Cinch spun and dropped into *seiza*. Mutt hit the floor on his back, hard, as Cinch's knees came to rest on both sides of the big man's head, next to Mutt's ears. He knelt like a massage tech about to lean into the upper pectorals of a patient.

Unable to breathe and sprawled on the floor, Mutt started to struggle up—until he felt Cinch's thumbs dig in at the corners of his eyes.

"You move and I'll pop your eyeballs out and step on them."

Mutt froze. Whatever chemical inbalance he felt wasn't strong enough to keep him fighting against that particular threat.

"Now, I'm going to get up and when I do, you can come to your feet. Take yourself over to the mediplex and let them look at you. If you don't, I will put you back down and out cold, and then I will haul your ass there over my shoulder. You understand?"

Mutt managed to nod.

"Okay. Get up."

Cinch snapped from the kneeling position to his feet, ready to move.

Mutt was done fighting. He stared at Cinch, rubbed at his mouth, sipped the air he wanted so much to reclaim. He turned away and walked toward the exit.

"Fuck," Brilly said, staring at Mutt. "Did you see that?"

Lobang glared at Brilly. "It was a trick. He suckered him."

Cinch wasn't breathing hard. He looked at the trio.

Tuluk smiled. "Would you care to join me?" he said.

Cinch nodded. He walked toward the table.

chapter 7

"Would you like another drink?"

Cinch shook his head. "No, thanks. One is my limit while I'm working."

"Smart, I like that. And your handling of Mutt was also very impressive." Tuluk sipped at his scotch, watching Cinch over the rim of the glass. He swallowed the liquid. "What brings you to Roget, M. Carston?" Tuluk made no attempt to pretend he didn't know who Cinch was.

"I believe it was a Durston Model Nine Star Cruiser," he said.

"How droll."

"The Stellar Rangers received a complaint from one of your neighbors, M. Tuluk." No point in him pretending he didn't know who the rich man was, either.

"That would be Gustav Kohl," Tuluk said.

"I'm not at liberty to reveal such information."

Tuluk shrugged. He had thin shoulders under the expensive clothing. "Do go on."

"The nature of the complaint required that we investigate. I am doing so."

"Ah, I see." He paused for a moment. "It must be difficult, flitting from planet to planet and mucking about in the criminal element." Another sip from the drink.

"It has its moments."

"I would think it a young man's game. Not that you're

old, M. Carston, but a man of your years must think now and then of retirement."

Cinch wanted to see how far he would go. "Now and then, yes."

"There's always room for a man of certain skills in my organization. I have been looking for a qualified security chief for my blueweed operation. It pays quite well, and the work is generally considered to be easy and safe."

Cinch thought Lobang might burst a blood vessel in his forehead when Tuluk said that, the guard's face was so red. Well. Not an outright bribe, he wasn't that foolish. And there was nothing illegal about offering a man a job when he retired from the service, either. But it told Cinch what he wanted to know.

Tuluk continued. "Even a frontier world has much to offer a man who is well-off financially. I don't know what a Stellar Ranger makes for field work, but I can guarantee a decent salary."

"What is 'decent'?"

Tuluk named a figure. It was about five times what Cinch could hope to make if he ever left the field and became a Sector Commander, close to ten times what he made now. It wasn't decent, it was obscene. Two years of that kind of money and he'd earn more than his grandfather had in his entire life. Certainly he'd never make that much honestly.

"I'm not quite ready to retire yet, M. Tuluk. But thanks for the offer."

"Well. Do think about it, in case you change your mind, M. Carston."

As he drove back toward Kohl's station in the borrowed car, Cinch did think about his conversation with Tuluk. There had been a time when he would have leapt on the rich man's offer so hard the locals would have thought they were having an earthquake. Money as a measure of success no longer interested him, however. He'd been rich himself, once upon a time. Not for long, but for a few days after he smuggled a load of contraband liquor to a planet where drinking was illegal, Cinch could have retired and lived in luxury had he chosen to do so. But even then he realized you could only live in one house at a time, consume so much good food and fine wine, sleep with so many beautiful bedmates. He'd enjoyed the game of beating the local law much more than he had the money he'd made for it. He'd pissed it away, the wealth, and never regretted it. Life was too short to spend it chasing fame or power or money.

No, Tuluk's offer didn't interest him, save in what it revealed about the man. The cattle baron and blueweed rancher had something to hide and the offer only confirmed it for certain. Now things would begin to get interesting.

There was a mostly-dry riverbed ahead, a short bridge spanning it. The road went through a series of hilly S-curves just before it reached the trickle that was the Sungai River, and the path meandered into a not-very-deep valley that sloped down to the bed. There were some hardy willow and cottonwoodlike trees along the dusty banks, as well as bunches of dark shrubbery and weeds with roots deep enough to suck moisture from the earth. As the local terrain went, this was practically an oasis, a virtual jungle compared to the surrounding plains.

As Cinch rounded one of the curves, he caught a glint of light from something in one of the bigger shrubs near the bridge. Probably nothing but a piece of junk somebody had tossed from a passing vehicle, a drink can or food wrapper. Easy enough to dismiss.

Then again, old rangers got that way by not dismissing easy things that might get them dead in a hurry.

Cinch slowed the car a little. Thought about what he ought to do. If he were wrong, if nobody was there, then he might look foolish—though nobody would see it. But if that stray reflection of hard sunlight meant he had company, then maybe he ought to check it out.

When he was out of sight of the river around a curve, he pulled the GE car to a halt, grabbed his rifle, and hopped out. It was easy enough to set the autopilot to follow the road at a slow speed, and he did so. He estimated how far away the bridge was, set the dash timer to kill the

engine's power about the time the car got that far, and sent
the empty vehicle on its way. Then he began to work his
way down the short hillock, angling toward the cover of
the trees further up the river. With any luck, he could stay
low enough to remain hidden from anybody on the opposite bank.

The GE car idled to a halt and settled to the road a hundred meters short of the bridge. Cinch had already made it
to the near bank of the river by then. He took a deep
breath and crouched low, then scooted across the river's
bed. The tiny stream of muddy water in the center was
narrow enough for him to jump without getting his boots
wet. Even so, the smell of moisture in the air was apparent, and it felt almost humid here compared to the arid terrain that surrounded the river. He worked his way to the
trees, then back toward the road. He wished he had his
camosuit, but by using the bushes and trees he was able to
keep to cover.

As he drew nearer the road, Cinch heard voices.

"So what do we do now, Pan? He just fucking stopped
in the middle of the fucking road—"

"Take it easy, Diji. Just wait a second and see what he
does. Maybe his car broke down."

"I dunno, man, I don't see him," came a third voice.
"Maybe he had a heatstroke or something and passed out."

"Seems awful fucking coincidental he would stop right
there," Diji said. "I don't like it. I say we scamper."

"Look, we didn't come to shoot the guy," Pan said. "We
just want to *talk* to him."

"That's good to hear," Cinch said. He moved out to
cover the three young men with his rifle. "No quick
moves, okay?"

"Fuck!" Diji said.

The trio turned to face Cinch. They wore handguns and
one of them had a hunting rifle on a sling over one shoulder.

"I can't believe you did that," Pan said. "Snuck right up
on us. So much for the dreaded raj who move like smoke."

Cinch grinned and raised the rifle so it pointed at the sky. "You'd be Pandjang Meritja." It was not a question.

The boy—he was maybe twenty, twenty-two standards—nodded. He was dark like his sister, but even with slightly coarser features the family resemblance was obvious. Pan was a little taller than Cinch, a bit heavier, well muscled. He wore desert camo, a wide-brimmed hat the color of sand, and hiking boots. Pan was the oldest of the three, as far as Cinch could tell. They appeared to have arrived here on foot. If they were afraid of him, it didn't show.

"That's me. Wanita says you wanted to talk to me?"

"Word gets around fast. You walk here?"

"We have horses tied a klick upriver."

"Why don't I move my car off the road and let's find a shady spot."

The one named Diji was too fair to be out in this kind of sun and Cinch smelled the aroma of sunblock on him. The other one, named Pohon, was something other than basic stock human, Cinch guessed. Pohon was short, squat, and had a slightly odd cast to his body and facial features. The oddness of his frame appeared to be from a slightly different joint and ligament structure. If that were the case, the genetic re-placement of his tendons gave him a somewhat better mechanical leverage than normal men. If Cinch's guess was correct, Pohon was a heavyworlder, able to survive in a couple of g's without major discomfort. He wasn't all that big, but he would be strong enough so he could probably upend a bus if he got excited.

After they hid Cinch's car in the trees, the four of them walked to where the three had tethered their horses. There was a wide spot where the stream filled a hollow, and the animals stood in or next to the water under the shade of a broad-leafed tree thirty meters tall.

"So, what do you want?"

"I understand you have had some trouble with M. Tuluk."

Pan laughed. "That's an understatement. How about, I hate his guts."

"You think he's a crook?"

"They'll have to screw him into his coffin when he dies. Soon, I hope. Me and the boys, we swipe stuff, mostly from Tuluk. Like mosquitoes buzzing a bull for all the harm we're doing. But Tuluk is big time. You know what they say. 'Steal a little, they'll put you in jail. Steal a lot, they'll *give* you the jail.' "

Cinch grinned. Pretty sharp kid. What he said was, unfortunately, true enough on a lot of worlds. Money talks, and big money talks the loudest.

"So, are you going give us trouble?" Pan asked.

"Not me. You're not breaking any galactic regs I know of, no civil rights violations. As long as you keep it local, it's between you and the constable."

All three of the young men laughed at that. Apparently they didn't have a very high opinion of Constable Maling.

They talked for another few minutes, asking and answering questions. They knew he'd come to answer Gus Kohl's complaints, they were sure Tuluk was the cause, and they'd help him if they could.

Cinch had found out what he wanted to know from these low-rate bandits. One more small piece in the puzzle. So far, it was shaping up to be fairly simple. He had the major players laid out, some idea of what was going on and why, and it was just a matter of time until he managed to fit the parts together properly to finish it. No sweat.

"Okay," the ranger said. "I just wanted to make contact and see where we stood. You stay out of my way, I won't bother you."

He turned to leave.

"Uh, Ranger?"

"Yeah?"

"Say hello to Baji for me?"

Cinch fought the urge to smile paternally at the young man. The tone of Pan's voice gave away a lot. Sounded as if Gus Kohl was right about what the bandit felt for Baji.

Cinch nodded, once. "I'll do that."

As he walked back toward his car, Cinch thought about

his upcoming vacation. He was due time off in a month or so. He should have this all wrapped up well before then. He was looking forward to kicking back and doing nothing for a few weeks.

chapter 8

"So, how was your visit to town?" Baji asked.

Cinch finished chewing on the bite of steak and swallowed it. It was a prime cut, cooked to medium-rare perfection. A meal like this would cost him a day's pay on any of the civilized worlds where meat was allowed, more where it had to be bought sub rosa.

"Interesting," he said. "I met a man named 'Mutt,' spoke to M. Tuluk, Wanita, and had a nice chat with her brother. He says to say 'hello,' by the way."

They were in the smaller of two dining rooms off the kitchen. A larger room for more formal dining affairs adjoined the smaller room.

Baji blinked and looked startled. "You saw Pan?" Something flitted across her face, some hidden emotion Cinch couldn't read.

Cinch nodded, busy chewing on another bite of the delicious beef. Sirloin? Or filet? One good thing about frontier worlds, they knew how to eat well.

"Well," she said. "He's nobody, just a boy who is going to come to a bad end, if you believe my great-grandfather."

"Do you believe him?"

"Sometimes. But enough about bandits. Tell me about yourself, Cinch. Are you contracted?"

Cinch took another bite of steak. Nothing subtle about

51

that change of subject. Baji had also changed her clothes since he'd seen her earlier. She now wore a sleeveless tunic and shorts, both in a pale orange silk. She had showered, washed her hair and fluffed it, and put on a new perfume. This one was less musky than the first one he'd noticed, more a flowery, peppery scent. The silk was thin enough so he could see she wore nothing under it. Her nipples were visible and her pubic hair apparent.

Hell, the voice he sometimes thought of as belonging to his baser self said, *why don't you just fuck her? She wants it, you want it. Who would it hurt? She's practically climbing on you. Go, boy!*

Cinch smiled at himself.

"Something funny?"

"No, I was just remembering something. Wouldn't make any sense to you. To answer your question, No, I'm not contracted."

She flashed her smile. "So, what did you find out? Is Gramp right? Is Manis—M. Tuluk—the one causing the problems?"

Cinch shrugged. "Too early to tell for sure. I would say probably, given his responses."

She toyed with the glass of wine in front of her. "What are you going to do?"

"Keep looking."

"What if you don't find anything?"

"I'll find something. I always find something. That's what they pay me for."

She shifted her position a bit, allowed her knees to spread a little, took a deeper breath and arched her back a hair.

Good Lord.

"Anything else I can get for you?" she said. "More steak or wine?" *Perhaps a little fellatio?*

"No, I'm fine," he said. But maybe not. Maybe this was going to be more of a problem than he thought.

"Did I mention that I have a little sister?" he said.

The air was oppressively hot, even with the sprinklers and buried root water lines going. Rainbows flared and faded among the fine mists from the sprinklers. Blueweed used a lot of water. Tuluk's private line ran all the way from Lake Hidjah in the foothills to the northeast, some hundred and fifteen kilometers away. Laying that pipe, a thick plastic tube big enough so a tall man could barely encircle it with his arms, had not been cheap, nor had it been fast or easy. It had cost two years, a million C's, four men dead in accidents, and dozens still drawing disability. Still, it had been worth it. The much-expanded blueweed crop had been thick and lush since. The entire cost of the water line would be amortized in another five years even if that was all he grew.

"Window up," Tukul said.

The limo's back window slid into place obediently, the polarized plastic going dark as the bright light splashed its way through the mists shrouding the tops of the crop. Even with the car's coolers going full blast, the heat had pounded its way through the open window. The compartment began to cool again, the damp-mowed-lawn smell of the blueweed faded a little.

"Take us to the Twist patch," Tukul said.

The limo's only other occupant was the driver. Lobang nodded. "Right." The limo lifted and began to move down the wide, plant-bounded lane.

Blueweed looked much like a corn plant, save there was no fruit and the broad, hand-shaped leaves and thick, pithy stalks were a uniform dusty blue-green. The plants achieved a height of five meters at maturity. They needed bright and hot sun through a long growing season, but also great amounts of water, two things that did not happen together very often on this planet. Where blueweed grew wild, it lived on the edges of lakes or rivers and only sparsely there.

Blueweed was the source of the most potent antibiotic in the known galaxy. In the proper dosages and mixed with appropriate secondary medicines, there were few bacteria, germs, or viruses that blueweed would not wipe out in vivo. More, the drug could be tailored to leave normal flora and fauna alone, thereby avoiding many of the side effects of most antibiological chems—such as fungal over-

growths and the diarrhea secondary to the death of enteric
bacteria. Almost nobody was allergic to pure blueweed;
with a little rejiggering of the basic formula, pathogenic
bacteria or viruses normally resistant to attack rolled over
and died nearly every time. It was truly a miracle drug. It
took ten liters of raw blueweed extract to produce four
cc's of the finished basic product, and one mature blueweed plant made about a half-liter of extract. It required
twenty plants for a vial of the miracle liquid, quite a lot.

Tuluk had twenty-five square kilometers of blueweed
under cultivation, more than sixty-five hundred hectares.
So he *had* quite a lot of the plants. A certain amount of the
crop was lost each season—ruined by spray-resistant insects, consumed by small animals, damaged by poor har-
vesting techniques and, of course, the necessary seed crop
that had to be left standing—but an average yield would
be worth almost two millions C's, before taxes and expenses. If all of his cattle vanished into thin air and his
other legitimate business interests fell flat, he would still
be able to consider himself a wealthy man. But not *the*
wealthiest man in the local system, or even on Roget. For
someone who wanted to be the wealthiest man in the *galaxy,* the cattle and blueweed and other odds and ends were
not enough. He needed something else.

Therefore the special crop. The Twist.

Tuluk smiled. The Twist would make him rich enough
to buy and sell planets, if he didn't do something foolish.

The rows of blueweed flashed past the semidarkened
window as Tukul leaned back against the biogel seat, custom orthomolded for his body. With this much at stake, he
indeed had to take great care. . . .

"—takes a lot of care," Gus said. He waved one hand at
the rows of blue-green plants.

Cinch nodded. The plants were about four meters tall,
still a month or so away from harvest. The leaves were
wet, the smell much like a freshly clipped hedge. Pleasant
enough.

"We water the roots more or less constantly," Gus continued, "there're seep-lines under each row. The mist we

have to do a couple times a day. Stuff likes the sun but it cooks if it gets too dry."

"Must take a lot of water."

"Yeah, it does. My crop is only a couple hundred hectares, that's all my wells will support. Tukul pipes his water in from Green Lake, up in the foothills."

"From the satmaps I saw, his crop is pretty big. It must require huge amounts of water. On a desert world, the water is supposed to be allotted, isn't it?"

"Yep. We have us a duly elected, five-member Hemisphere Water Board, all right. Thing is, Tuluk clears a million easy every year on his crop, that's not counting what he makes from his beeves. A member of the HWB makes about thirty thousand C's before taxes, just about enough to feed, house and clothe a small family. Three of the members of the board live in big expensive houses and fly very nice vehicles. You don't have to be a hydrologist to know which way the water flows, son."

Cinch smiled. "I don't suppose you'd have a horse I could borrow?"

"Sure, but you're welcome to use the car all you want."

"There are places where a man on a horse is a lot less conspicuous than one in a powered vehicle. And places where a mount can go that a car can't."

Gus grinned. "Why, son, it sounds as if you plan to do some sneaking around. I ought to tell you, Tuluk's land is all pulse-posted."

Cinch shrugged. "Appreciate the thought, but I'm a Stellar Ranger, after all. You don't think I'd trespass on private property, do you? That would be against the law."

"I hear you," Gus said.

The more you knew, the better off you were, Cinch figured. He stood in the stable next to a big rawhide mare that Gus said was one of his best mounts. He'd already cinched the heavy leather saddle in place—another advantage of frontier worlds, they usually didn't use plastic for their saddles—and was now strapping a set of saddlebags behind. Gus had lent him a carbine scabbard and he had his rifle shoved into it.

The mare sniffed at him a couple of times, took an apple from his hand and managed to spatter him with the juice as she ate it, but she seemed comfortable enough. Cinch wasn't an expert when it came to horses or kuda or other such ridable animals, but he knew enough to let the mount know who he was and get used to him before he tried to climb aboard. The mare—Gus called her "Mada," which meant "honey" in the local dialect—didn't seem bothered by him. Which was good, since they were going to be together for the next few days.

Cinch had his map reader packed; the little flatscreen had showed him that the bulk of Tuluk's property was nearly a two-day ride on horseback. It might take a little longer than that, since he'd be moving cautiously and not in a direct line. It would be good if he and the honey mare got along.

He checked his camping gear once more before he sealed the crow strip on his bags. Solar water still, tab-meals, heat thread blanket and spare batteries, solar recharger, com unit, small medicomp. He had plates of ammo for his pistol and rifle, a small sealed videocamcorder and a camo spidernet tent. He could have packed a lot more, but he liked to travel light.

It was early, just past dawn. He heard her come in behind him and turned to see Baji standing in the stable doorway. She wore a transparent nightgown and a not much thicker robe draped loosely over it. Hardly something to be wearing outside in the chilly morning. He felt the cool air's touch beneath his synlin windbreaker.

"Where are you going?"

"For a ride."

She blinked, still half asleep. "When will you be back? Can we have lunch again?"

"Sure."

He swung himself onto the mare's broad back, settled his boots into the stirrups, and urged her to turn with a light pressure of his knees and a gentle tug on the left rein. The mare responded easily, danced back a couple of steps to line them up with the door, and moved forward. She knew he wanted to go out, he didn't need to do anything else. If he did his job, she seemed to say, she'd do hers. Good.

Cinch felt a little guilty about not telling Baji that their lunch wasn't going to be today or tomorrow or even the day after that. But not very guilty. He wasn't her father, her brother or her lover, he was just the ranger come to do his job. Everything else was secondary.

He rode off into the cool morning.

chapter 9

There were no natural moons hung in the skies over Roget, so the nights were relatively dark despite the thicker sprinkling of stars here nearer the galactic core. Too dark for a man on horseback to be risking his mount's legs against pooger holes or sand spits. While the days of having to shoot a horse because she had a broken leg were past—veterinary techniques could have a leg bonded and workable in a few days—it would be a long walk back to Gus Kohl's station from where Cinch was now.

Insects buzzed past in the darkness, mostly on their way elsewhere. Fortunately this world did not seem to have the local equivalent of mosquitoes. He wore a buzz-repellor to keep away any other bugs who might find him tasty.

Cinch lay wrapped in his blanket on a pad of branches cut from a stunted tree that seemed to be halfway between greasewood and Ponderosa pine. The heat threads of his blanket kept the chill away, and his saddle served as a hard pillow. Honey grazed nearby, hobbled so she wouldn't go far. He had eaten a pull-tab meal, not the best dinner he'd ever had but filling, washing it down with fresh water he'd raised from the seemingly dry ground with his solar still an hour before sunset. The mare had drunk her fill from the plastic tub; he'd washed his face and hands and sponged off his body with the rest before dumping it. He had a canteen for the morning and he would stop and distill another five or ten liters during the day as needed. Most people didn't realize just how much water there was to be had in the desert, were you properly equipped.

He had the camo-tent laid out next to him, just in case he needed to cover up, but he didn't think he'd need it in the dark. He was still a day's ride away from Tuluk's property, out in the middle of nowhere. It was very peaceful out here, far from civilization. One of the benefits of being on a frontier world, the quiet of the desert at night, just you and the sky unblemished by city glow—

The mare whinnied suddenly and shuffled her feet. Out in the darkness, something hissed. Something with a lot of air to use in making the sound.

Cinch pulled the rifle from the scabbard next to the saddle and flipped the blanket off. He had removed his boots to sleep, stuffing them with his socks to keep out unwelcome visitors, but he didn't bother to put them on. His guess was that one of the local predators, an ularsinga, had come to pay him a visit. If he'd had a fire, the lizard would probably have steered well clear of him, but he didn't want to risk being spotted by a passing aircraft so the campsite had been kept dark. He did have a powerful halogen lamp, however, and he picked it up as he moved toward the mare.

Honey nickered nervously and snorted at the unseen creature that was probably stalking her. She shied toward Cinch. "Take it easy," he said. "Nobody is going to hurt you."

The hissing came again.

Cinch marked the direction of the sound and pointed the lamp that way. He dialed the beam to wide-angle and flicked it on. A ragged triangle of desert lit up brightly, the rocks and plants throwing hard-edged shadows as the light splashed the dark ground. There, twenty meters out, the red gleam of a pair of widely spaced eyes reflected the beam back at him.

The horse saw that and didn't much like it. She snorted yet again and backed away.

Cinch dialed the light to a narrower focus.

The lizard was big, pushing three meters, though a third

of that was the long tail it lashed rapidly back and forth. It hissed again, showing pointed teeth as long as Cinch's little finger.

He held the light steady with his left hand and laid the rifle's barrel over that wrist. He pressed the sight tab and the tiny red dot lit, floating a couple of centimeters over the weapon's receiver.

"Shoo!" Cinch yelled.

The lizard flattened to its belly but didn't move.

"Go on, shoo! You can't eat my horse!" Cinch yelled at the ularsinga.

He didn't particularly want to shoot it. He was far enough away from anything that he didn't think the shot would be heard by anybody, but a dead lizard would draw other predators, probably before daylight, and he didn't relish having to drag the thing several hundred meters away from his camp in the dark to keep them elsewhere.

"Go away, dammit!"

It must be very hungry not to flee. Most wild animals would run from men, especially if they'd had any experience with humans and their weapons.

The lizard turned to look off into the darkness to its right. It hissed again.

Crap. Maybe Cinch could throw a rock at it and drive it off—

Something else hissed in answer, something that sounded as if it was damned near on top of Cinch.

Oh, shit. He recalled the briefing, now. The things sometimes hunted in pairs.

Cinch twisted, swung the light around, saw the second ularsinga bounding across the sand toward him, mouth open. The thing's tongue was a pale pink, the inside of its mouth almost fish-belly white. It was maybe five meters away and moving much faster than he would have thought it could. He had maybe a second before it got there—

Cinch put the red dot on the thing's tongue and fired.

The recoil flipped the barrel up as the plasma roared into the night, burning much brighter than the light he held—

The oncoming lizard tumbled, flipped completely over

onto its back in a half somersault. The end of the tail came down and smashed the light in Cinch's hand, shattering the sealed-beam bulb. With the after-image of the plasma blast making him half blind already, the loss of the lamp didn't help any.

The wounded lizard thrashed about, throwing up clouds of sand, hissing and making a kind of piglike squeal as it fought a losing battle with death.

Cinch leaped away to avoid being flattened by the thing. Close, too goddamned close—!

Then the sound of the other lizard's rapid footpads squeaking through the sand reminded the ranger that he was still in trouble. Shit! He turned toward the sound—

Tuluk didn't usually stay out in the fields this late, but the Twist was special enough to warrant his attention. Inside a shed made to look just like all the other tool and storage sheds scattered among the blueweed fields, his tame scientist, Picobe, was trying to explain why the yield wasn't going to be as high as expected. Tuluk wasn't happy to hear it. Behind them, outside the camouflaged bunker, Lobang stood leaning against the limo, watching the springdog on its deadly patrol.

Picobe's voice droned on. "—nitrogen fixing nodules are somewhat stunted due to secondary yeast infestations. Of course we can compensate for that, but the absorption of the fungicide slows the normal rate of photosynthesis by partially blocking leaf surface area and naturally that inhibits the . . ."

Tuluk tuned the voice out, watching the springdog as it rolled by.

The name had nothing to do with the way the robot looked. It had a head of sorts, but the shape was more like a steel leg-trap mounted on the end of four linked hydraulic pistons and rods. The brain was in the main trunk, which was shaped much like a garbage can pounded flat on the bottom. The machine rolled on eight small independently axled and powered rubbery tires that could extrude small spikes for added traction, allowing the thing to climb a bare rock wall were the incline not too great. The tracks it left in soft ground were a giveaway, being that the robot weighed almost two hundred kilos. The big drawback to using it as a mysterious cattle killer was that somebody had to run around behind it brushing out the tracks or there was no mystery. Still, it was fast, deadly, and could be programmed with basic guard-and-hold or attack-and-destroy patterns. A good tech could override the no-human-target governor built into the biobrain at the factory and this particular model had been rigged to go for anything or anybody Tuluk sicced it on. It was an expensive toy, the springdog, but it had its uses. Men who would charge into the muzzle of a shotgun without a second thought would sometimes go white and back off at the sight of a biomech dog. There was something enervating about being *eaten*, even by a machine.

"—therefore the third-generation plants will bell-curve somewhat—"

"Picobe, stop prattling on and give me the bottom line here. In language I can understand."

The scientist, a short and rotund man with a red Botany Guild tattoo encircling his left arm from the wrist to the elbow, blinked and went into what looked like a computer search mode. "Uh, well. At best, you're only going to get half the next crop fully psychoactive, maybe a quarter more partially so."

Tuluk thought about that for a second. "Nothing you can do to improve on that?"

"As I have just explained M. Tuluk, no. With the following generation, maybe a 15 percent improvement, generation after that, 8 percent more. It drops off sharply after that. In time, perhaps . . ."

Through the open doorway of the shed, Tuluk watched as the springdog rolled silently past, bioelectronic senses searching for prey. Lobang shoved himself away from the limo and followed the thing. He amused himself by tossing pebbles at the robot. The little rocks clacked or clanged or thunked, depending on where they hit. The robot paid the hard rain no mind—there was no danger from it and therefore the pebbles could be safely ignored.

So, what Picobe was saying was that the best yield he

could hope for on the Twist a couple of seasons from now was around three-quarters of what was planted. That was acceptable. Tuluk would simply plant more. That had been the intent all along. After all, who would be able to tell that the Twist was anything other than ordinary blueweed? That was the whole point in having these expensive scientist types, wasn't it? Try to hide ropa plants in a field of tomatoes and any one-eyed yahoo in a spotter craft could see them. A drooling idiot with spectroflex scanners could tell the difference between legal moster and highly illegal kuning almost from orbital heights, even though they looked very similar to an untrained observer. But the Twist looked exactly like blueweed because it *was* blueweed, save for the invisible chemical/genetic factory installed within it. It was a perfect disguise.

"What about the new refinement procedures?"

"There is no problem there. The lyserje component scans, the bacterial carrier splice accepts the infective viral matrices as designed and engineered. Dosage is stable and consistent at three hundred micrograms."

"You have samples of the latest batch?"

"Yes." Picobe moved to a nearby table, pulled a small jector vial from the rack there. The tiny plastic tube had a covered pressure popper on one end. Thumb the cover off, press the popper against human flesh, and it would blast the chemical within through the skin for a subcutaneous delivery. The altered blueweed was the Twist, the genetic parent and incubator, but this was the final product. It had a number of crude, if colorful, names applied by its users: Oh-Oh-Oh!, Throb, Breathe-O, Cumagainandagain. While it was not addictive in the physiological sense, nobody who tried it ever wanted to quit after one dose. According to those who had enjoyed the experience and had something to compare it to, it was the ultimate sensual drug. It gave the user almost thirty minutes of more or less constant physical pleasure, orgasmic intensity arising from even the simplest act. Tuluk himself had never had any desire to try it, but it was potentially worth billions to him. Maybe trillions.

"Good." He slipped the vial into his pocket.

To Lobang, Tuluk said, "Stop that."

The big man turned to look at Tuluk. "Huh?"

"The springdog is worth more than you are. Why are you throwing rocks at it?"

"It doesn't hurt it none."

Tuluk shook his head. God.

He glanced at the chronometer built into the cuff of his tunic. Almost 2350. He had better get back to the station, he had a special visitor arriving soon.

To Picobe, he said, "All right. Continue your research. Lobang, get the limo."

As the vehicle lifted, Tuluk looked at the Twist patch. There were only a few hundred of the special plants now, but that number would increase dramatically in the next few years. As would his income.

He spared the springdog a final glance as it patrolled, protecting his investment. Good doggy. And it never pissed on the carpet, either.

Cinch couldn't see the oncoming beast but he knew it was close—the ground shook from the thing's approach. He'd dropped the useless light, and the rifle's after-image muzzle blast had left him still mostly blind. He knew what he had to do to survive—the trick was, could he do it fast enough?

He jerked the rifle down to his hip, pointed it straight ahead into the darkness and fired. A hit would be a small miracle, but he wasn't trying to hit the lizard.

Once again the bright flash lit the night, turning the darkness into a lightning strobe of day. Just long enough for him to see the charging ularsinga. It was almost on top of him—

The night reclaimed them. He wouldn't have time to aim. He pointed the weapon from memory and pulled the trigger as fast as he could, once, twice, three times—

The lizard hit him, knocked him sprawling. He tried to hold onto the rifle, lost it as he tucked and rolled out of the fall. He hit the ground hard on his right shoulder, tumbled up too fast to stay on his feet, fell again. The second roll stopped when he hit body of the first lizard.

Damn!

Cinch scrabbled up, reached for his pistol, realized it was not on his hip. He'd left it next to his saddle. . . .

He stood there barefoot and unarmed in the dark for what seemed like a very long time before he realized the lizard wasn't coming at him any more.

When his breathing had slowed and his eyes had cleared some, he went to his pack and found the spare lamp.

His frantic hip-shooting had worked. The charging ularsinga had been moving too fast to stop, even though it was dead by the time it got to him. The top of its head was gone; one foreleg had been shattered and nearly blown off. He'd been lucky. Using the muzzle flash of a rifle to see in the dark was an iffy deal at best.

Cinch found the mare and brought her back to camp. He put her bridle on and wrapped it around a tree limb. He packed his gear. Easier to move the campsite than to try and drag the dead lizards away. Besides, there was too much blood soaked into the sands now to stay here.

He moved carefully in the dark, watching his steps. Well. At least the bodies of these two ought to attract and keep the rest of the local fauna fed long enough for him to get some sleep before the sun came up. He'd have to pay a little more respect to these reptiles in the future. They were tougher than he'd thought. Then again, he was still alive and the two lizards weren't, so he was tougher than they had thought, too.

chapter 10

At midmorning the sound of an approaching aircraft made Cinch pop the camo-tent. He draped it over himself and the mare and held still as the high-flying vessel passed. The tent was mottled in the four most common colors of the local sand, as near as his color-coder could program it. From a few hundred meters, he ought to look like a splotch of terrain, nothing more. The silk was refractive-threaded so it would diffuse his heat signal some. It probably wouldn't fool an expert with a scope looking specifically for a man, but it might pass a hurried scan. There were a lot of hot rocks under the desert floor.

The best disguise was for them not to be looking, though. So far, he didn't think they had any reason to think he was out there.

When the aircraft was past, Cinch reloaded the tent launcher and spent a few minutes with the still collecting water for the mare. He would be at the edge of Tuluk's eastern cattle range by dark, according to his map comp.

The horse drank, less than she would have liked. He didn't want her overwatered.

He looked at his radio transceiver; saw the screen dotted with the distant, multiple signals of cattle transponders. They were weak this far off, just a hint of the feedback-locate wave registering. Invisible fencing, it was called. It was a simple technology. A cheap, throwaway solar-powered-battery-backup transponder was stapled to the skull of every animal when it was young. With the computer transmitter on-line, no normal animal in the herd would step past an unseen line. The transponder would give it a painful jolt to turn it back if it tried. Instead of cowboys or dogs or fences, a computer told the cattle where to go and when. An expert operator could do wonders with properly tuned equipment. Once, on Livona, a cattle baron had his herd of more than two hundred thousand animals spell out a WELCOME sign visible from orbit for a visiting rich uncle.

A dry riverbed loomed. Cinch had spotted it on his map and he made for it, intending to use it for cover for the next few kilometers.

On the far horizon to the west, a gray line of clouds was barely visible. Given that these were the first such clouds he'd seen since he'd been on this planet, Cinch paused. Since he was planning on using the riverbed, it was best to check. He dialed up the government weather channel, got the local map.

Well. A front was moving in. Forecasters were predicting scattered thundershowers in the late afternoon and early evening.

That could be good or bad. A nice rainstorm made excellent cover, played hell with electronic detectors if there were any, gave people a good reason to stay indoors, cut down on visibility. Then again, riding in the rain wasn't the most pleasant experience, and there was always the danger of flash floods in low-lying areas. A mixed blessing, but maybe moot since it was hot and sunny at the moment and the clouds were a long way off.

Cinch moved into the dry riverbed.

Tuluk allowed himself to sleep late, then stayed in bed another thirty minutes after that. He seldom indulged himself in this kind of thing, but after last night he was both exhausted and quite pleased with himself. After his second wife died, his interest in women had abated considerably, but now and then he felt the old urges claim him. It was good to know that he could still perform with the stamina of a much younger man, when it was necessary.

It had certainly been necessary last evening. He was drained absolutely dry.

Tuluk grinned and arose, padded into the fresher and into the shower. She'd only stayed a few hours but that had been more than sufficient, especially given the stimulus of the Twist extract he'd given her. One of her orgasms had been so powerful that her arching up with it had literally lifted him clear of her and into the air. Amazing.

As the hot water beat down upon him, Tuluk found himself singing the Andorean Planetary Anthem. He laughed aloud at himself. They'd been playing that the first time he had been with a woman. He could remember both the tune and the woman as if the event had been hours past instead of decades. He wondered whatever had happened to that delightful young fem. He had been a callow boy, just off his first cattle implanting, she was somebody he'd met in a pub. She probably went on to become a prostitute— she'd certainly had the skill for it. She had ridden him like a wild horse, and they hadn't slept for the entire night. She knew things he had never even heard about, much less imagined doing. Ah, youth.

He lathered and washed the suds away, praising in song the bravery of the Andorean Legion as it fought to save the world from the villainous Privateer Fleet. When he got to the part with the rockets rising and lancing forth, he knew exactly how they must have felt. . . .

Cinch rested in the shade of a stunted bush, allowing the mare to wander and graze as the still gurgled and filled the plastic water trough. He watched a small brown lizard raise and lower its head rapidly, the red wattle under its neck puffing up and deflating like a small balloon. It was stalking some unseen prey in the shade. The lizard crouched and darted forward. After a moment, Cinch saw the wriggling bug, some kind of beetle, held in the triumphant lizard's jaws. The little reptile moved off into the deeper recesses of the bush's shade to enjoy his meal.

It was quiet, peaceful, the rainclouds having drawn nearer but the heat lightning in the distance not producing any thunder he could hear yet. A cool breeze blew along the river's bed, stirring the dust, bringing with it the scent of rain coming. It might be hours away, but it would arrive eventually.

Cinch grinned. Sometimes he thought about leaving the rangers, finding a sparsely settled world like this one, settling down. He could run a small ranch, find a good woman, get contracted, maybe even raise kids to chase the chickens around. It was a pleasant fantasy, it held a certain allure. No worries about lawbreakers, no more having to chase all over the galaxy dropping into gravity wells that were usually sand holes or damp jungles. No more wondering what the strange planet's morning would bring, no fretting with the knowledge that the last sunset you'd seen might truly *be* your last one.

Cinch laughed, and the mare turned to look at him.

Yeah, someday, maybe. When he was old and slow and a waste of his badge and gun. For now, the danger was the spice in his life, the newness of each planet the seasoning that made it all worth tasting. Somebody had to do it and he was good at it, as good as anybody who wore the insignia. Yes, it was a test of a man or woman's mettle to be a ranger, but life wasn't about safe harbors, at least not until you got too old to sail the seas. Someday, if he lived long enough, he'd hang up his gun and badge and walk off into the sunset, but not just yet. Not today.

The trough was almost full and Cinch went to fill his canteen before the mare began slobbering into it. Someday was off in the future. The here and now was what mattered. Living too far in the future or the past could get you in a lot of trouble.

Lobang leaned against the porch support, chewing on a mouthful of toasted hazelnuts. He didn't appear to hear Tuluk coming.

"The ranger is gone," Tuluk said.

The bigger man straightened and looked at his boss. "Huh? Gone? Gone where?"

"That's the question, isn't it? Why don't you go and find out where? I don't pay you to hold up my front porch."

"How could he be gone? Brilly didn't call, he's watching the road."

"He's on a horse, Lobang. You don't have to stay on the road if you ride a horse."

The man stared at him. Tuluk answered his unasked question: "If I depended on you and Brilly for my intelligence reports, I'd be in lizard shit up to my hairline, wouldn't I?"

Lobang said nothing. Another small blessing.

"Get the hopper and start a spiral search of my property."

"Damn, boss, that'll take *days!*"

"I don't care if it takes *years,* do it. There's a Stellar Ranger riding around out there somewhere. Not knowing where he is and what he's up to could cause me a great deal of trouble."

"What do you want me to do when I find him?"

"Just find him, first. We'll worry about what to do after we figure out where he is and what he's seen."

Lobang shambled off and Tuluk stood watching him. This ranger was tricky. He could screw things up. That couldn't be allowed to happen, no matter what it took to stop it.

chapter 11

The mare had been around cattle; their sounds and scent didn't seem to bother her. Cinch had spent enough time himself among such beasts so he was also used to them, though the smell of damp dung mixed with the dust kicked up by their hooves didn't do much for him.

Some of the cattle had found their way to the thicker vegetation along the riverbed. A few lay in the shade of the trees with roots deep enough to stay green, a few munched on plants in the bed itself. Most of the rest of the herd, probably three or four thousand head, wandered along eating scrub and tufts of brown grass that grew fairly densely nearby. It was an open range, bounded by nothing more than the natural landmarks like the river and the electronic fencing each animal carried.

By now, Cinch rode along the edge of the river, out of the bed. The thunder that announced the coming rain had grown louder in the last hour, and a fresh trickle of muddy water flowed along the center of the once-dry river. The rain fed the thin stream from upriver, and while a strong man could easily jump the shallow runoff at the moment, that could change in a hurry. Cinch had seen flash floods before, had once watched a sudden wall of frothy brown water surge through an arroyo on Deet's World and catch a startled springbok before it could get away. It would be embarrassing to drown on a desert world. Not only would he be dead, but the rangers would be shaking their heads and calling him stupid for a long time when they got together and swapped stories.

Hey, you remember old Carston?

Yeah, what a dupe. Drowned in the middle of the fucking desert, can you believe that shit? Jeez, what could he have been thinking? Shit like that makes us all look bad, you know?

No, if there was a sudden flood, Tuluk might lose a few unwary cattle but the rangers weren't going to lose one of their own if Cinch could help it.

As if to punctuate his thoughts, the first drops of rain began to fall, fat and heavy, raising small clouds of dust where they hit and spattered.

While he hadn't expected rain when he'd started out, Cinch had been on enough strange planets to carry gear for the unexpected. He dismounted, pulled a hoop-and-film protectant from his bag. The device was simple enough in construction and easy to use. Unfold the hoop—a memory-plastic circle that opened to about two meters in diameter—fill the reservoir tank with the liquid film, shake, and wait five seconds. The film would begin to rise from the rim like smoke. You caught the top edges, twisted them together, pinched off the excess, and you had what looked like a huge version of a child's soap bubble wand. Hold the hoop over your head, parallel to the ground, and drop it. It would coat your hat or hair and everything under it with the film. Before it had a chance to set, you wiped your face to clear it from your nose and eyes and mouth; thirty seconds later, you were waterproof. The material was one-way osmotic. It would let perspiration out but no water in. The film had a half-life of two hours and would be completely gone in twice that, broken down into harmless and mostly organic components. If the rain had not stopped by then you could reapply it, you could find a spot dry enough.

The drops were still few and far between as Cinch passed the hoop over himself. He wiped out patches over his eyes and nose and mouth, poked holes for his ears. He thought about trying to protect the mare but decided against it. Unless she was used to it, trying to get her to step through a—for a horse—tight-fitting hoop might be more trouble than it was worth. He did use a patch to cover the mare's head and ears, though she shied at the touch of the nearly invisible stuff. His gear was mostly protected, but he pulled a few more sections of film and covered his rifle and saddle. Best he could do.

Just in time. The skies opened up and the fat raindrops were joined by pellets of hail, some of which were as big as the tip of his little finger.

Film or no film, this could get painful. He looked for shelter, avoiding the few trees. It would hardly do to get blasted by lightning.

There was no other cover in sight and he thought briefly about setting up the tent. It was big enough to cover him and the horse easily.

But the hail stopped in a minute; and while the rain pounded down heavier, blowing almost horizontal in gusts, that was bearable. Water began to pour off his hat brim, a thin stream that fell onto his jacket and ran down his back. There was a spot near his groin on the inside of his left leg he'd missed with the film, and it almost immediately soaked up whatever water found its way there. Never failed but that he managed to miss a place. Damn.

Lightning struck a tree three or four hundred meters away. Cinch happened to be looking right at it when it hit, and he saw in the strobe several cattle flying from the force of the strike. Cows weren't real bright, they always seemed to gather under whatever lightning rod happened to be around and suffered the consequences for it. The thunder boomed. The mare tried to dance away, but responded to his firm hand on the reins.

With the rain sheeting and blowing as it was, he lost most of his landmarks. Cinch pulled the navigational compass and managed to get a fix on his intended direction though the water beading on the small screen. He turned away from the river and urged the horse forward. The wet spot on his pants grew a little bigger and colder.

Ah. The glamorous life of a stellar ranger. What could compare to this?

He grinned and the rain spattered against his teeth.

"No offense, boss, but we're wasting your fuel out here," Lobang said. "And my time, too."

Tuluk looked at the comscreen. Lobang's image shook, despite the cam's steadigyro. The window of the hopper behind Lobang ran with long streamers of water, and the clouds behind that were dark and roiling. It was a bad day to be flying and Tuluk was glad it was Lobang and not him out there in the hopper.

In his office, he could hear the rain pattering down on the sound roof he'd had installed just last year. Thin sheets of tuned metal over his office and bedroom allowed the sound of the too-infrequent rain to drum into the house, a natural rhythm Tuluk found most enjoyable.

"You don't have anything better to do," Tuluk said. "And fuel is cheap. Keep looking."

He couldn't hear it, but he could see Lobang sigh and start to shake his head. "You're the boss."

"That I am."

He reached out and shut the com off. This storm was a big one. If the ranger was out there, he was either holed up somewhere or getting wetter than a barrel of fish. Not likely he'd be doing much damage. Chances of Lobang spotting him were slim, even with sensory gear. Nothing like a little lightning and rain to fuck up IR or UV spotting scopes, not to mention what it did to doppler.

The rain tapped at the special sounding board, lulling him. Perhaps he'd been worried unnecessarily. For all he knew, the ranger could be washed away by now, a glitch in history whose drowned body would be picked clean by the ularsinga and cow buzzards. And when the rangers sent somebody to find him? Too bad, he would say, he seemed like such a nice fellow. And if he survived, well, there was still the offer of a job. That could be made more lucrative, certain bonuses could be mentioned. Every man had his price and certainly he could afford one ranger.

The drumming sped up, slowed, then the plate made a

sound as if a handful of gravel had been tossed at it. More hail, likely. A little of that wouldn't hurt the blueweed, it was a sturdy plant. A few stalks would be blown over if the winds gusted high enough, mostly around the edges of the fields. This rain was just what he needed; it would clear the dusty air, give the land a fresh and clean look.

Tuluk reached for his drink, sipped the smoky scotch. He found it hard to worry when it rained like this, always had. Safe, warm, dry in his house, it was difficult to feel too threatened by one man. True, it didn't hurt to be cautious, but then again there was no point in being a little old fussbudget, either.

He listened to the rain's percussive song.

Cinch dismounted and walked in front of the mare, leading her over the now-muddy ground. The footing was bad, and if somebody was going to step into a hole, better it was him—his legs were a lot sturdier than the horse's. The storm had been pounding at them for more than an hour with no signs of letting up, and it was dark enough so that pulling up or stopping the mare from a misstep while he was mounted might be iffy. Better to walk and see the terrain than to ride and not.

A few minutes earlier Cinch had spotted a mother ularsinga leading a trio of her young to higher ground away from their water-filled burrow. If the big reptile had seen him she hadn't let on, just hustled her babies up a slight rise toward a stand of wind-blown bushes.

Of the cattle herd there was no sign and he hadn't checked the transponder readings lately. The air had a slight ozone odor in it, probably a lightning hit somewhere close. This proved to be the case when, a few hundred meters later, Cinch and the mare passed a shattered tree. The fresh tan of the inner wood gleamed wetly. Big splinters lay around, including a couple stuck into the ground like spears. The lightning had boiled the sap instantly and, having no place to go, the superheated liquid had blown the tree apart like a hand grenade. Two cows lay on their sides next to the tree, and the smell of burned meat had not quite been washed away by the downpour.

The horse wanted no part of the tree or those who had stupidly sought shelter under it. Cinch didn't blame her. They veered away.

The blueweed field lay just ahead, another hour or two's walk even at this pace. It would be night by then; and if somebody stumbling across him in the rain was unlikely, then the same thing happening in the rain at night was less so.

The film was still holding, save for that wet splotch on his pants that looked as if he'd peed on himself. And so far, he hadn't seen anything worth comlining home about. He wasn't even sure what he was looking for, except that in the same way that a terrier knows a rat, he would know it if he saw it. Maybe there was nothing *to* see. He shrugged. Even so, that meant something. The more you knew about your quarry, the better.

Through the sound of the steady rain and gusty wind, there came another sound: an aircraft. Cinch stopped. The sound was almost right over him, very close. He'd never get the camo-tent out in time.

Cinch blinked away rain and tried to pinpoint the sound. If somebody were below the rain ceiling, he or she ought to be worrying about a wind shear that would smack them into the ground. And what kind of idiot would fly below the ceiling? If they were above the ceiling, they probably wouldn't be able to see him if he shot off a whole magazine of flares.

He saw the hopper, though. It went past no more than a hundred meters to his right and about that high, moving diagonally away from him. The hopper was a good-sized vessel, a ten-seater, with fans and repellors thrumming at full power. As he watched, a blast of wind hit the craft and shoved it to within fifty meters of the ground. The pilot compensated, the fans roared louder, and the hopper shot up into the clouds. The engines rumbled for a little while, then faded.

Damn. What the hell were they doing? That was stupid flying, sure enough, very risky. Anybody with half a brain would know better than to pilot aircraft in this kind of weather unless he had to. And—had they seen him?

He doubted it. When no sounds but rain and thunder reached him for the next half hour, Cinch felt better, though.

"No sign of 'im," Lobang said. "I circled the Twist patch three times."

Even though the comlink was coded and shielded, Tuluk winced at Lobang's use of the name. The man's mouth had to be bigger than his brain.

"All right. It'll be dark soon. Might as well come on in."

"Sir."

The rain had finally begun to ease up. The musical drumbeat on the roof had slowed and grown quieter. Well. As far as the ranger went, there was nothing to be done for it. In the clear light of morning, he'd have Lobang go looking again.

Cinch reached the edges of a blueweed field about the time the rain slacked to a halt. Good thing, too, the film on his clothes was starting to peel and flake into powder.

The rows between the plants were wide enough to drive a small flitter, so keeping the horse far enough away from the leaves to avoid being soaked was easy. Interesting stuff, blueweed, from what he had gotten in his briefing about it. And if what Gus had told him about Tuluk was even close, the man could spend more money than Cinch made in a year each and every day for the rest of his life and never notice it. What, he wondered, what cause a man with that kind of disposable income to want more to the point where he would try to drive his neighbors away to get it?

Cinch directed the mare around a particularly deep-looking puddle ahead of them. Guessing the motivations of others was always a problem, especially rich people. It wasn't, in his experience, only that they had more money than the rest of the galaxy, it was also that they did think differently.

Ah, well. That wasn't his problem. Let the headshrinkers worry about such things. His job was to enforce the

law; more, to enforce the *spirit* of the law. Figuring out if
the laws were being broken was the first thing to be done.
Stopping those infractions, if indeed they were such, came
next. *Why* was important, of course, but for a ranger that
sometimes didn't come in until later.

Keeping the horse out of the next puddle was more important than any of it at the moment, though. Cinch paid
his attention to their path. One step at a time.

chapter 12

"Boss, somebody broke into the supply shed in the Southwest Quadrant. They ripped off a bunch of stuff and trashed the rest."

Tuluk sat at his dining table eating breakfast. Thin beefsteaks, rare, an omelette made from a dozen quail eggs, panfried *bortol,* a kind of tuber that looked and cooked like hash brown potatoes but tasted like a cross between apples and carrots. He chewed on a bite of the omelette and nodded at Lobang. "How did they get past the alarm system?"

"Power went out during the storm. Every other alarm on the station went off. I sent crews to shut 'em down and by the time they got to the Southwest the thief had come and gone."

"That would be our friend Pan Meritja," Tuluk said. "The little twit."

"You don't think it was the ranger?"

"No, I don't think it was the ranger. He might break in to snoop around, but why would he steal anything? Or trash the place?"

"To make us think the raj did it."

Tuluk blinked at Lobang. Damn, an answer that actually made sense. The sense of well-being he'd felt during the storm turned sour. The food on his plate suddenly seemed too much. He pushed it away.

"Take the hopper and go look around that area. Tell Brilly to take a flitter and go check on the Twist."

"The springdog is there," Tuluk said. "It'll take care of anybody not in its recognition circuit."

"Just tell Brilly to go look."

Lobang shrugged.

When the comsat was in just the right location to give him an added security on his shielded pipeline, Cinch put in a quick call to Gus Kohl.

" 'Morning, son. Where are you?"

"I'd rather not say. I just wanted to let you know I'm taking good care of your horse."

"Got a little wet, I expect."

"A little. I'll talk to you later."

Cinch folded the com and tucked it away, broke his fireless camp. He had used the camo-tent, now configured to the color of the weed, and he packed it and saddled the mare. It had been passing damp, but the sun was already drying the air and plants, not a cloud in sight.

As he rode along, Cinch stayed alert for any sound of air or ground craft. The blueweed made for a dull vista. It all looked the same save for the occasional stunted plant or broken stalk. Now and then some small animal would scamper across the lane ahead of him, and he could hear its chittering as he passed. The air held the cut-grass smell he'd noticed in Kohl's field. He supposed there were worse ways to spend his time than riding horseback on a still-cool sunny morning, far enough from civilization so that it might as well not exist. It made him wonder what the pioneers might have felt out here, knowing they were very nearly alone in all this empty country.

"Any sign of him?"

"No, sir," Lobang said. "We've crisscrossed the Southwest Quadrant like a Denseweb spider. If he's there, he's invisible and the same temperature as the ground."

"Where is Brilly?"

"He's at the Twist shack. Nothing there."

"Keep looking."

Tuluk shut the com off and stepped into the shower.

As the day wound down toward darkness, Cinch began to think about finishing this trip. So far, he hadn't seen anything worth worrying about. He'd found and explored a couple of shacks set in the weed, nothing unusual about the small buildings. The blueweed seemed to go on forever, given his circuitous route. A flyover would have given him a broader picture, but he'd wanted to poke around at eye level. You sometimes saw things that way you'd never notice whipping past at air speed.

Cows and crops, that was all that was here, and Cinch had had about enough of both by now. He didn't know what he'd expected to find, but there weren't any contraband nuclear weapons plants or corrals full of slaves. Too bad. That would have made things more black or white, easier to deal with.

When it got too dark to see anything else, he'd make camp again. Tomorrow he would head back toward Kohl's station and see what else he could think of to do.

"He's still out there," Tuluk said.

"How do you know that, boss?"

"I know. Keep looking."

Cinch had given the mare a slack rein and she was ambling along when she stopped. Her ears flicked forward.

Cinch stared into the darkness. He couldn't hear anything, save for the odd insect buzzing past and a slight stirring of the weed under a small breeze.

The horse snorted and backed up a couple of steps.

"What is it, Mada? What's out there?"

Nothing.

He swung himself off the saddle and dismounted. Pulled the carbine. "We got us another lizard, girl?"

He felt rather than heard the thing approaching. A vibration in the ground, something heavy. Something on wheels. It was in the lane ahead of him, not showing any lights.

Cinch got a quick flash of memory: Gus Kohl's prize bull, strung out in chewed flyblown bits.

Springdog!

Cinch moved fast. There was a plate of armor-piercing ammo tucked away in his saddlebag. He dug around for it.

The sound of the dog's motors came, a thin hum growing louder. It hadn't begun its attack-mode yet, it was still checking him out. Wouldn't take long, though—

The mare snorted and danced backward half a dozen steps.

"Damn, hold still!" Cinch lunged after the mare. Without that AP ammo, he was in trouble. The dog was plated and effectively bulletproof against ordinary hunting rounds.

The hum of the dog's motors cycled up.

Now it was in attack-mode. It would be on top of him in ten seconds—

The horse turned and bolted.

Fuck!

Cinch ran from the lane between two rows of the blue-weed. He forced his way through the plants, banging the rifle and his arms on the thick stalks.

Behind him, the springdog came on. It would probably be programmed for a direct attack on an intruder. Therefore it would try to follow him. As powerful as it was, it was much too wide to plow through the weed easily. That should slow it down some.

Cinch dodged, plants thumped against his body. He could likely outrun the thing as long as he gave it plenty to run over, but sooner or later he would get tired. The dog wouldn't. It would chase him until it caught him. And if it didn't catch him fairly quickly, it would shift into a tracking rather than a chase mode. It would move up and down the narrow lanes, positioning itself, waiting. A self-contained biomech like the dog could run for weeks before it needed recharging.

Shit.

* * *

The call woke Tuluk from a sound sleep. He grabbed the com. "This better be good," he said.

It was Brilly. "M. Tuluk, the springdog is chasing somebody out in the weed."

Tuluk sat up. "Who?"

"I dunno, I ain't gone to look yet."

"Well, *go* look, idiot!"

Tuluk slid from the bed and hurried to get dressed. He paused long enough to com Lobang, who'd also been asleep judging from the sound of his voice.

"Huh?"

"Get dressed. The springdog is chasing somebody at the Twist patch."

"I'll get the limo," he said.

Cinch had to get back to the horse and those saddlebags. Already he was winded, and smacking into the heavy stalks and leaves of the blueweed wasn't doing him any physical good, either. He worked his way back toward the main aisle, hoping to catch up with the mare.

Behind him the springdog flattened more of the plants in its way. It was gaining.

As Cinch managed to clear the weed and regain the lane where he'd left the horse, the rifle caught a stalk crossways. He was moving fast and the weapon was jerked free.

Oh, *man!*

The dog was almost on his heels. He couldn't stop to retrieve the carbine.

He sprinted in the direction of the horse, unable to see her. They could probably outrun the thing if he could get mounted in time. But she could be half a klick away by now.

Behind him the dog cleared the weed and achieved the aisle.

Cinch slid to a stop. He'd never outrun it on flat ground. The rifle was gone, the horse too far away to help. It was going to catch him unless he went back into the weed. But if he did that, it would catch him pretty soon, anyway. He was already tired.

Fuck.

"Brilly? Brilly, answer your damn com!"

In the back of the limo, Tuluk, his shirt still hanging outside the cor-line of his trousers, tried to raise the guard.

Lobang had the limo moving at speed.

"Why the hell doesn't he answer?"

"Probably gone to help the springdog," Lobang said.

"Damn, damn, damn! Can't you go any faster?"

"Topped out now, Boss. Don't worry. We'll be there in ten minutes."

Cinch spun to face the springdog. Almost without thinking he snatched his pistol from its holster and brought it up to a two-hand hold. The starfish slugs would flatten like blobs of clay on the dog's armor, they wouldn't even slow it down—

The dog was ten meters away and coming fast.

Wait. Wait—!

The eyes!

Mounted next to the steel jaws, one on either side, were the cameras that let the dog see. The lenses were inside an armored tube, but the photomutable gel itself had nothing but glass plates directly in front of them—

Cinch put the sight dot on the left eye and fired three times as fast as he could.

The first shot missed clean. The second shot hit the jaws and *spanged* away harmlessly.

The third shot split on the armored eye tube; he saw it splatter. Enough of the bullet went into the lens to rupture the gel.

The dug spun toward the left. Stopped. It would compensate in a second, switching all input to the remaining cam.

Cinch's instinct told him to turn and haul ass as fast as he could. Find his horse and ride the hell away.

But while the dog was stopped and recovering, it wouldn't take long to jigger its program.

Instead of running away, Cinch ran toward the dog. When he was a meter away, it turned back toward him.

The first shot was dead on. It blew out the other eye. Cinch put both his remaining rounds into it to be sure.

The dog froze. Motors whined. It would be switching to sound pickup now, but springdogs were programmed to work visually. It could hear him if he made any noise, even track him that way, but in theory it wouldn't attack because it wasn't set up to do so by sonics. Its computer recognition program wasn't that good.

Cinch found he'd automatically pulled a spare magazine and reloaded his pistol. When he dropped the empty, the springdog oriented itself toward the sound of the mag hitting the ground.

The ranger backed slowly away. It heard him and turned, but did not move.

"Freeze, dickhead!"

Cinch jumped a meter to his left, turning in the air as he moved.

The thug named Brilly stood five meters away, pointing a pistol. He fired, and the sound and muzzle blast seemed to be aimed right between Cinch's eyes. But the bullet zipped past, missing.

Cinch shoved his own pistol out one-handed as if punching with it. He fired.

The slug took Brilly high on the right side of the chest, almost at the shoulder. He spun away from the force of it, his pistol flew. It didn't look like a fatal wound, no major organs there but it put him down. He started yelling, cursing.

Cinch started forward to help the wounded man.

The springdog beat him there.

Cinch emptied the rest of the magazine at the dog but it was a waste of time and ammo.

Apparently somebody had overriden the springdog's visual-attack-only program. There was nothing in the universe that could save Brilly. The sound of human flesh and bones being torn and crunched filled the night. Brilly stopped cursing.

Cinch turned away, feeling sick. He found his rifle and hurried to find his horse while the blind springdog finished its grisly work.

chapter 13

"Well? Did you find Brilly?"

Lobang nodded, his face grim. "What was left of him."

The two men were in the Twist shack.

"What are you talking about?"

"Something happened, I can't tell what exactly," Lobang said. "The springdog jumped Brilly. It came at me, I had to use the fry-circuit code to failsafe it. The dog'll need to be reprogrammed. And it looks like it needs new eyes, too. Ain't nobody gonna be fixing Brilly, though."

"What about the dog's memory?"

"Might be able to pull it up, might not. The fry-circuit is not a good way to shut the system down. You almost always get major damage."

Tuluk said, "Damn. When Brilly called, he said the dog was chasing something in the weed. Why would it turn on him? And what was it chasing?"

"I dunno the answer to either of those. If the dog was chasing something, it ain't out there now. If whoever it was could turn the springdog around and sic it on Brilly, he knows a fuck of a lot more about biomechs than I do."

Tuluk refrained from saying anything. Whatever else Lobang might be, he was more familiar with the operations of the springdog than anybody else locally. This was not good.

"All right. Get the dog repaired, see if you can get a recording from it as to what it saw. Get some men out here and take care of Brilly's body. He have any family?"

"A couple of sisters in the East Hemi."

"Send them his pension, tell them he died in an accident. Fell and broke his neck or something. Have our medic fill out the proper forms."

Lobang nodded. "You think it was the raj?"

Tuluk stared into the warm darkness, listened to the wind rustle the blueweed. "They're not that clever."

"I guess that only leaves one guy it could be, huh?"

Tuluk nodded. He was afraid so.

Cinch had passed better nights. His flight through the blueweed from the biomechanical dog had given him the beginnings of a dozen bruises on his arms, shoulders and torso, as well as his legs. His ribs were sore on the left side, his left wrist ached from when the rifle had been twisted loose from his grip, and he'd pulled a hamstring in the panicky sprint. His right ankle had what felt like a mild sprain. Every time the horse took a step it jolted something. It wasn't so bad now, but after he'd had a day or so to stiffen up, he was going to want to lie down and not move for a long time.

Nothing like running through what could pass for a thick grove of small trees at full steam to remind a man of how stupid that was. Given the other option, he had really had no choice, but it had cost. Maybe he *was* getting too old to be out in the field.

He had a jector of painkiller in his medikit and if it got much worse he'd use it, but for now he gutted it out. Somebody would find the dead man and wounded springdog, probably sooner rather than later, and he needed to be far away with his wits—such that they were—as clear as they could be. The warm fog of painkiller would make him feel better physically, but it would also slow his reactions and make him stupid. He couldn't afford that.

He changed lanes a number of times, angling away but not heading directly back toward Kohl's station. Rather he moved north. There wasn't supposed to be anything in that direction for several hundred klicks except more blueweed and mesa. If anybody started looking for him, they probably wouldn't think he'd go that way.

The ground was still wet, but the lane was a mix of dirt and springy blueweed mulch and didn't seem to take a hoofprint very well. He was glad of that, not only for the lack of a trail but for the relative softness. Once he got back to hard ground, it was going to jolt him a lot worse.

Now the question that loomed large in his mind:

Why would there be a springdog and a human guard out there in the middle of nowhere? True, he hadn't seen anything, but you didn't drop the kind of money a biomech cost just to leave it running around for no reason.

Tuluk had something there he wanted to hide. Bad enough to leave a biomech programmed to kill to protect it.

That was *very* interesting.

"Nothing," Lobang said. "I got our men covering the ground like a blanket and if he was here, he ain't here now."

Once again in his office, Tuluk nodded. "All right. Call them off. It's been almost three days. He's had plenty of time to get off my land."

"The pulse fence didn't show him come in."

"Jesus, Lobang, any nitwit with a cheap radio com can rascal a pulse fence. The damned thing is only supposed to let us know if a stray with a bad transponder steps past it. I would imagine a Stellar Ranger has access to enough technology to slip a fence undetected, coming or going."

"Yeah, I expect you're right."

Tuluk shook his head. "Anyway, it doesn't matter. He'll be going back to Gus Kohl's station. We'll wait and see what happens after that."

"You're the boss—"

Tuluk cut him off. "I know that. You don't need to keep telling me."

Cinch was, unfortunately, right about how he was going to feel once his bruises had time to set. The assorted pains were bearable without resorting to drugs, but the time on horseback was not in the least bit pleasant. By the time he got back to Kohl's, all he wanted to do was lie down in a tub of hot water and sleep for a week or two.

But he took time to brush the mare and give her a bag of whatever local grain she was used to before he went into the house.

He met Gus as he used the shoe caddy to pull his boots off just inside the door.

"You look like ten klicks of bad road, son."

"Feel like it, too."

"Have a nice camping trip?"

Cinch nodded. "Real interesting. I feel pretty sure the rangers are going to be able to help you take care of your problem."

"Glad to hear it."

"Meanwhile, I think I'm going to take a shower," Cinch said.

"There's a rojowood soak tub behind the house, under that little gazebo. You're welcome to use it."

"Thanks. I believe I will."

Cinch went to his room and dumped his gear. He stripped, took a good look at himself in the mirror. He had more than a few bruises, some of which were already shading from brown to yellow at the edges.

He wrapped a big towel around himself and went to find the soak tub.

The gods surely must have built a special palace for the person who invented hot water, Cinch thought. He was stretched out almost full-length in the oval tub, his head resting on the edge, one hand gripping the side to keep him from sinking. Vapor rose into the evening air, which was warm itself. Oh, man, this felt good. He couldn't imagine anything else that would feel quite this great at the moment.

"Hi," Baji said.

Cinch twisted his head to one side and saw her standing there, also wrapped in a towel. As he watched, she unwrapped herself and stood nude under his gaze. She smiled.

He had seen better-looking women, he was sure; he just couldn't remember when or where at the moment. There wasn't a blemish on her, she was young, beautiful, and very aware of both. She gave him a good, long look.

"Mind if I join you?"

Before he could speak, she moved to the tub and climbed the little ramp. Her pubic hair nearly touched his nose as she stepped down into the hot water.

Oh, great.

Baji eased herself into the water until she was directly across from him, settled down on the seat so that her nipples were level with the surface. Must be sitting on her feet, he decided. The water should come up to her neck on that side of the tub. She leaned back, face toward the evening sky.

"Ah," she said. Then she looked at him. "And where have *you* been for the last week?"

"Camping," he said.

"Camping. I thought we were going to have lunch."

"Next time it rolls around, if you want."

She pouted or pretended to. "Around here it's not considered polite to take off for six days and not tell people where you're going."

"Sorry. Part of my job."

She bobbed up, brought those perfect breasts clear of the water for a beat, then settled down lower than before. The thin stream of bubbles from the spa machinery made anything under the surface mostly invisible. Just as well.

"Find out anything interesting?"

He shrugged. "Not much. It's a big country, lots of open space. Not a lot going on."

"Gramps said you looked like you'd fallen off a cliff. That's an ugly bruise on your shoulder."

"Sometimes I'm clumsy."

Something touched lightly the inside of his thigh, very near his groin. It was so faint that he thought maybe he imagined it. Despite the usual effect hot water had on him, what he'd heard referred to as the "boiled noodle effect," the nearness of this very attractive and very naked young woman was somewhat ... stirring.

"I wouldn't have thought that," she said. "That you were clumsy. I heard about the fight in town. I heard you moved better than Lobang does when he fights."

The touch came again, a little higher. Definitely not his imagination. Another centimeter and her foot was going to discover Cinch's own personal version of a rapidly lengthening flagpole.

Yes! All right!

No. Not a good idea. Remember what we promised Gus?

Fuck Gus. After you fuck her, of course.

Not a chance.

You really are getting old, Cinchy. Lost your nerve.

It was time to get out of the water, all right. But doing so right at the moment would certainly show Baji that the effect she wanted was, in fact, a reality. Cinch tried to think about other things. Icebergs. Snow banks. The Tasmanian Flu. None of which seemed to help.

"Baji," came Gus's voice.

She frowned and looked toward the house.

"Baji, you out there?"

She didn't answer.

"We're over here," Cinch called back. "In the tub."

If looks could kill, Cinch would have become a radioactive scum floating on the surface of the hot water.

Gus ambled over. "Ah. There's a call for you. Madeline. She says you were supposed to let her know about the alterations on the boots."

Baji looked disgusted. "I forgot."

"She's holding."

"You could have brought me a com."

Gus smiled. "I forgot."

"Tell her I'll call her back."

"You see a sign that says 'lackey' on me?"

Her eyes flashed and she stood.

Cinch was careful not to look directly at that glorious backside as she stepped out of the tub, grabbed her towel, and hurried off. She moved quickly, and it was obvious she was angry.

Gus looked at Cinch.

"Thanks, Gus."

He nodded. "I figured you might be a little too worn out to deal with her. Better get to your room before she finishes her call, though."

"I'll do that."

"And you might want to lock the door, son."

Cinch nodded again. And prop a chair against it, too.

chapter 14

Cinch lay in the bed, too tired to drop off. He thought about Baji, about her youth; and while he didn't have the energy to smile, he wanted to. He could remember back to his youth.

At twenty, Cinch Carston was invulnerable. He would stroll through the killing zone of a Gorn ghetto at midnight and smile at the cutters sharpening their talon gloves. Nobody ever bothered him. The smugglers he ran with thought he was crazy. The Gorns thought so too, and that's why he wasn't sliced to bloody ribbons. A cutter he met in a bar once, who'd seen him on his late night walks, told him:

"Humanboy cakewalkin through de zone all by heself, aigh? The uncles, deh figure he not right, he eyes too bright, he walk too springy. Not drugbrave, he, but crazybrother humanboy. Any two, three uncles, deh can rake him down, the uncles deh know dis, but—who gonna be first uncle in de chute? Crazy humanboy must be carryin' somethin' maybe bomb, maybe some disease, maybe de crazy, it catchin' and deh don' wanna get it."

Cinch had laughed when he heard the story. He wasn't crazy. He just figured when your number came up you got called, and until it did why worry?

At twenty-two, he made the Dimple Run with Wormy Rogers and Deluxe Antoon. With half the system police laying traps and the other half chasing them, they'd threaded the needle and got clear. The three of them risked their lives to smuggle six cases of Henry Weinhard's Private Reserve to Dryworld, where drinking was a mortal sin punishable by beheading. When they split the profits after expenses, they each earned about three hundred C's. Almost as much as the basic dole on Rimrock where they started the operation. They laughed all the way home.

At twenty-five, while Cinch was spending a little time in the outworlder jail on Kuhara for smuggling in sexual toys to the pasha's second-level harem, Cinch was braced by Dogman Belvedere, who had been put into the cell by friends of the pasha to teach the smuggler a lesson in humility. The Dogman had nine confirmed kills in hand-to-hand combat. Six of the legendary Dogman's kills were legal, these being ronin gunning for his reputation or he for theirs. Three deaths were more questionable; and while there was not enough proof to indict him, the conventional wisdom thought these three murders-for-hire. In addition to the nine confirmed, rumor had it that Dogman could notch the handle clean off a big power pistol with his unconfirmed kills if he wanted to, not counting the legions of maimed but not dead people he had created. The Dogman was nobody to fuck with.

When the Dogman stepped into his cell, Cinch knew exactly who he was. The Dogman was a head taller, ten years smarter, fifteen kilos heavier and supposedly fearless.

Three seconds after he entered Cinch's cell, Cinch put the Dogman down with a sweep, then kicked his head hard enough so the meanest man on the combat circuit slept for a week.

When he woke up, the Dogman retired from competition.

At thirty, Cinch Carston tracked and hunted down the Ordinian Axe, the worst mass murderer in recent galactic history, six hundred and forty-seven known victims on eight planets in twelve years. At the final moment, the new ranger found himself barehanded against the Axe, a giant of a man who deadlifted GE cars for exercise. He took the Axe's weapon—which was actually a machete—and buried it in the man's belly. The Axe was certifiably insane and there never would have been a trial, he would have gone straight to the nearest bughouse for life. Cinch didn't think that was fair to the victims.

So as he lay in bed, thinking about his recent encounter with Baji, he was too tired to smile but he thought about it. He wasn't a coward. But he was older and maybe that meant he was a little wiser and a little less foolish and he had learned one thing:

A man could get *hurt* messing with the wrong women.

As he'd expected, Cinch woke up sore. Not that he had slept all that long or well. He felt as if he were a couple hundred years old and had spent the last century or so rolling down a rocky mountainside. Maybe he was getting too soft for this. Maybe it *was* time to pack it in, find a rocking chair on a porch somewhere and watch the grass grow.

He managed a grin through the pain. It wasn't like he'd never been bruised before. He'd be okay once he got moving and loosened up a little. At least nobody had picked the lock to his door—nobody meaning Baji—and hopped into bed with him. He had a certain amount of resolve, sure enough, but if that beautiful creature he'd seen in the hot tub had sneaked into his room naked when he felt as miserable as he had last night, he would surely have taken some comfort there. He wasn't that old.

It was early, dawn not quite ready to take over from the darkness. Baji seemed to be a late sleeper and with any luck, he could be away from the house by the time she got up.

He chuckled to himself. Big, heroic ranger, running from a little girl. Better to have drowned in the rain-swollen gully and be laughed at by his fellow peace officers than let *that* get out, despite his reputation. In the rangers, it was always a case of "What have you done lately?" Everybody had old war stories.

He climbed from the bed, went into the fresher and attended to his bodily functions, ran a hot shower that helped him feel a little better, and dried off.

Now what, O professional investigator? How are you going to find out what it is that Tuluk thinks is so valuable he's willing to kill to keep it hidden?

As Cinch stretched a little to loosen the tight muscles in his back and legs, he considered the problem. It was surely illegal, whatever it was, and that might narrow things down some. What could you hide in a big field full of blueweed?

Well, truth be told, a lot of things. A couple billion in gems would be easy enough to bury. Guns. Drugs. Stolen electric components, flashchips and the like, would take less room than emeralds or diamonds. Pirated software . . .

No, that wasn't the way to go, there could be all manner of things stashed out there in the fields.

Cinch finished stretching and examined himself in the mirror. He looked like hell, all bruised and scratched, but felt some better. He could survive without doping himself. He had an idea that he didn't want to dull his wits—however sharp they might be—as long as he was on this world. Too many people seemed to want him fucked—one way or another.

Interesting that a man as rich as Tuluk would risk it all by doing something really illegal. Oh, sure, wealthy men cut corners, they could be unethical and competitive to the point of really nasty and most of the ones Cinch had run into were, to a degree, but when you were so rich you'd never be able to spend it all, what was the point in trying to gather more if you had to step that far over the line?

Then again, Cinch knew the thrill of the hunt, the joy of the chase, and that wasn't about money. Maybe Tuluk was in the criminal business for the rush it gave him. Men had done stranger things.

As he dressed, he thought of other ways he might go about his investigation. The pot was probably stirred sufficiently by now. Maybe he would go into town and have breakfast there. His resolve about Baji was strong, but then again he wasn't made of steel.

"What now, boss?"

Tuluk leaned back in his chair, steepled his fingers, and looked at Lobang. "I want somebody stuck to the ranger like a field tick. Get some people he hasn't seen. I want to know if he belches, and if he does I want a recording of what it sounds like. If he appears to be calling in the troops or sending signals that could imperil our operation in any way, he is to be stopped."

"But I thought you wanted it to look like an accident—"

"I didn't say kill him, I said stop him. Clonk him on the head and bring him here, whatever, we can figure something out. I don't think he knows anything dangerous yet. We must see to it that he does not learn such things."

Lobang nodded and left.

Tuluk worried over it like a cat with a bit of tough meat. Things had escalated past where he thought they would. He thought he was still all right, but doubt had raised its hairy eyebrows at him and it bothered him more than a little. He liked to be in control, liked to have the pawns move under his command. This ranger was a wild card and Tuluk did not like it in the least. He would have to do something. He would have to find out exactly what the man knew and what he planned.

What, after all, was the point in having all this money and power if he couldn't exercise it?

Then again, if the truth must out, this was all most stimulating. He hadn't felt quite this alive in a long time, you didn't count the recent bedroom escapades. It was fun to play—as long as he won.

Morning found Cinch cruising toward town. There were a couple of restaurants there, one that didn't look too bad. Given that there was a choice and not many tourists to keep them in business, one of them ought to be fair. Local people could stay home if it wasn't.

The ranger picked the smaller of the two places, not far from Wanita's. It was Everlast plastic, but somebody had painted it a flat white and put a sign over the door that said MELINDA'S.

Inside was a counter with stools and a dozen tables. The smells of beef and eggs and some kind of flat bread or cake baking blended into a nice aroma. The grill was behind the counter and a thin woman stood at it, cooking. Another woman, younger and more corpulent, did the waitressing. There were twenty people eating, talking, or waiting for breakfast. Most of the tables were full. A good sign.

Wanita sat alone in a corner, sipping coffee or whatever passed for it here. She saw Cinch come in.

"Hey, Ranger. Come have a seat."

He smiled at her and nodded, moved to sit across from her.

"Haven't seen you in a while," she said. "Been busy?"

"Doing this and that, yeah."

The waitress came over, put a thick white mug full of steaming coffee in front of him without asking. He nodded at her. "Thanks."

"You want breakfast?"

"Sure. Whatever Wanita's having."

The waitress bustled off and he turned back to Wanita.

"How do you know I'm not having pig guts or fishheads or something?"

"You can eat it, I can."

She laughed. "I like you, Ranger."

"Cinch."

She sipped at her coffee. "My brother kinda likes you, too, though he'd break his arm before he would say so. He any help to you?"

"Some. He seems like a good kid."

"He is. Would have been better if he'd never gone to work for Tuluk, but it's a small town. So. What's on your horizon?"

"Little more poking into things."

She grinned again. "Yeah? Any particular kind of things you poking into?"

Cinch blinked. Was that a double entendre? Easy enough to find out. He said, "Wherever I might fit."

"I have some thoughts about that," she said.

"Oh?"

"How hungry are you? For breakfast, I mean?"

"I could miss it, there was something better to eat."

"Why don't you come to the pub with me? My living quarters are off the back. See if we can find something for you to poke into or nibble on."

It was Cinch's turn to grin. A grown woman, very attractive, one who not only found him so but was willing to act on it. He couldn't think of a better offer, bruises and scratches notwithstanding. He pulled a ten MU coin from his pocket and dropped it on the table to pay for their breakfasts and coffee. Came to his feet as smoothly as he could manage and extended one hand to her.

Cinch always thought high praise for a person's body was that they looked better without clothes than with them.

Wanita looked better nude than covered, and that was saying something. He told her so, and she was pleased. She was lean, had a dancer's musculature, smooth skin the same color as her face. Her breasts were small, with dark chocolate nipples, her pubic hair a dense thicket of blue-black. She stripped without modesty and helped him shuck his clothes before they moved to the bed.

They kissed, touched each other gently at first, explored each other with hands and lips and knees and then everything else.

Cinch quickly found out that Wanita's nickname of "magic mouth" was well deserved, and she found out a few seconds later that it had been some time since he had been with a woman. A couple liters ago, Cinch felt, somewhat embarrassed. But she laughed and it was fine and not even a little bit messy.

Thus warmed up, they exercised considerable affection

and skill upon each other, so that each of them reached a peak twice more in the next hour, a third time in the hour following.

If Cinch had been tired and sore before, he was nearly comatose by noon. And he couldn't remember a time better spent, in more than one sense of that word.

Lying side by side and exhausted, they held hands.

"Not bad for an old ranger," she said.

"You're pretty good for an old pub owner yourself."

They laughed.

"Thanks," he said. "You are quite delicious."

"Don't thank me, I got as good as I gave." She shifted a little, pressed her hip against his.

"Forget it," he said. "I'm an old ranger and I'm done."

She laughed. "So, how goes the investigation?"

"Slow. I have some ideas but I'm kind of easy to keep track of. Tuluk is having me watched, makes it kind of hard to sneak around."

"How can I help?"

"Well. I don't know that you can. But your brother might be able to do something."

"If it would cause Tuluk any grief, all you have to do is ask."

He smiled, put his hand on her hip and stroked her. "Could you get word to him to contact me? My com is probably leaking big, but he could leave a message with you if that would be okay."

"No problem."

She rolled over onto her side to face him. Ran one finger along a scar on his arm he'd never bothered to have revised. "Big adventure?"

"Nah. Cut myself shaving."

"My. Here, let me show you something." She moved down.

"Wasting your time," he said.

"I like a challenge."

Normally Cinch didn't like being wrong, but it didn't bother him at all this time. Magic, indeed. This woman was practically a miracle. When he got ready to buy that ranch and raise kids, he was going to come back here and look her up. Assuming he ever got the strength back to be able to stand up and leave . . .

chapter 15

Would that this business were all he had to worry about, Tuluk thought. But, no. There were a hundred other items that needed his personal attention each and every day of life. A man who sat at the head of a multimillion-standard empire could not simply sit back and let his underlings handle all the details. Such a man would quickly find himself being robbed blind or extended into places he would rather avoid.

His computer, having been given the proper instructions, set up priorities each morning. There were calls from bankers, legals, suppliers, and others with whom he did business, calls that must be attended to to keep his connections patent. There were orders to be signed, moneys to be dispensed, legally and otherwise—bribes went a long way toward keeping the machinery of his business lubricated—decisions to be made that only Tuluk himself could make.

He paced in his office, giving his computer secretary verbal instructions. Would that this ranger and his vast potential for interrupting the new income via the blueweed Twist were his only worries. Why, could he turn all his attention there, the matter would certainly be resolved quickly. But rich and powerful men had large responsibilities that could not be shirked.

"—tell Wiggis Awan at Offworld Export that his offer

is too low by half," Tuluk said. "Put it in the proper form."

"Sure thing, honey," the computer's voice said. She had been programmed to sound like a holovid star from Tuluk's youth, a sultry woman who had been the wet dream of billions of teenage boys for probably thirty years. He wondered what she looked like now, or if she were still alive. Better to keep the fantasy and not know, he decided.

"Tell Diba Akang that I am expecting the delivery of my responder order on time or I shall certainly invoke the penalty clause and he can kiss his profits good-bye. Phrase it just so."

"Right, babe."

"Put in a call to Vice President Wither and arrange for a lunch date for my visit to the capital next month."

"Anything you want, sweetie."

"And tell him no Subbonesian food this time; that crap makes my stomach burn."

"No Subbonesian food, got it."

"Order a case of my single-malt scotch from Bernard's and tell them I want it within a month this time."

"Scotch, within a month, yes sir, honey."

Tuluk paused in his pacing. "What's next on the list?"

"Dogmatics has some question on the warranty for the replacement parts ordered by M. Lobang for the biomech."

"Some question? To hell with that. The damned springdog failed to perform as advertised! They'll make it good or I'll sue them!"

"Gee, baby, I hate to point this out, but according to your personal and private record, the biomech was altered beyond factory specifications and therefore the warranty is, technically speaking, void."

Tuluk nodded to himself. Ah, yes. Wouldn't do to have a representative of the company showing up here to argue the point now, would it? The ranger would be all over him like flies on fresh dung.

"All right. Cancel that. We'll eat the cost."

"You're so very clever, Manis."

Tuluk grinned and shook his head. How many billions of men would have given their left nut to have the woman whose voice was his secretary comp say that to them? Being rich had its compensations. Money might not buy you love, but it sure could buy you something that looked and felt and tasted just like it.

"Okay. What's next?"

Cinch's walk to his borrowed car was slow but a lot looser than it had been before he and Wanita had been together. He grinned as the afternoon sun tried to cook him. Sorry, he thought, I feel too good to be bothered by a little heat.

As he drove back toward the ranch, he worked out the beginnings of a plan. Strictly speaking, what he intended wasn't legal. Hell, what he intended was as crooked as a Teleganian pirate; still, that line between the letter of the law and the intent of those who had made the law did get real blurry. Nobody knew that better than a ranger who had to interpret the difference in places where a hammer or a microscalpel might be the only tools you had. As long as he could get up and look at himself in the mirror without flinching, Cinch figured he wasn't doing too bad as a translator.

Baji flounced into the kitchen as Cinch dug through the cooler looking for something to eat. She was not in the best of moods.

"I thought we were going to have lunch," she said, her arms crossed tightly.

"I don't recall that was supposed to be today," Cinch said, pulling a packet of thinly sliced steak from the refrigerator.

"Where have you been?"

It was all he could do to keep from laughing. Last night he'd locked his door because he was worried this little girl might sneak in and try to have her way with him. Last night was a million years away, now that Wanita had squeezed him as dry as a sponge left outside in the bright sun for a week.

"Working. I'm a ranger, remember. I had some sources I needed to see in town."

"And was one of those 'sources' Wanita the slut?"

"I thought you liked her."

"I was just trying to be polite. You shouldn't waste your time on her, she doesn't know anything that can help you."

Wrong about that, Cinch thought. *I can't remember when I was helped so much. And my time on Wanita was anything but a waste.* But he said, "That's for me to determine, Baji. I know how to do my job."

"She's not what she seems, Cinch. Don't say I didn't warn you!"

With that, Baji flounced out of the room.

Cinch grinned. It was hard to remember how much he had wanted to play games with her only a few hours ago. Wanita certainly had dulled that particular edge for him. Baji seemed much more like a spoiled kid than she had when they were naked together in the hot tub last night.

Cinch went back to his search for food. He needed it.

Tuluk's day wound down.

"Incoming call from M. Ulang," his computer said. "Shall I cycle it?"

"No. I'll talk to him. Level One security scramble."

"Sure thing, sweetie."

Ulang was an alias, of course, and probably the man was having his end of the conversation routed through three or four bounces so anybody trying to trace the com wouldn't have a prayer of doing so.

Ulang was the dope dealer who was going to fatten Tuluk's wallet beyond his ability to haul it around without a trailer rig.

"Ah, M. Ulang. So good to hear from you."

"M. Tuluk. How's the weather?"

"Tolerably warm. You know how it is."

The conversation, which would run along these lines for another five minutes or so, was nothing but a cover. The real communication was already over, a speed-pulse of subsonic electronic code scrambled and one-time-only, now safely recorded in the flash memory of Tuluk's computer. Anybody without Tuluk's retinal pattern, the name of the first dog he'd owned and his EEG pattern wouldn't be able to call the file up without wiping it; and even if they could manage to circumvent the wards, they wouldn't be able to decipher it without the resources of a major cryptography lab and several weeks of effort. By which time it would be moot. All the message said was where and when M. Ulang would arrive on this world, and that was going to be in the next few days.

M. Ulang and Tuluk had business to transact together. Major business, and neither of them wanted anybody else to know squat about it.

The conversation finished, and did it have a listener who somehow managed to overhear it, it would have sounded fatuous in the extreme. Tuluk had long been of the mind that anybody who listened to, or followed around, almost anybody for an average day would probably think them deranged. Such had been his experience when he'd viewed surveillance recordings or read reports filed by various of his spies. A man came out of his residence, walked to his flitter and drove away. Half a klick later he turned around and went home, alighted from his vehicle, reentered his house and stayed there for the rest of the day. What could have been on his mind? Or a woman being followed in a large market went up and down one aisle six times looking for something. Was she blind? Stupid?

Ah, well. It did not matter.

He entered the proper codes, allowed his eyes to be scanned by the security system, his brain to be graphed, and after the message pulse was expanded and decoded, got the gist of the conversation with Ulang: the man would be arriving in three days and he would meet Tuluk at the agreed-upon site, itself deliberately kept from this message. The place was the Flathead Mesa, a rock formation that looked like its name, some two hundred kilometers from Tuluk's ranch house. It was in the middle of no-where, the mesa, and thus the choice. No one was apt to sneak up on a man conducting business there—not unless he were invisible, too cold for IR gear to spot, and quiet as a flea in stealth boots. The time for the meeting was 2400 hours and any traffic out at midnight would be visible to the horizon to the watchers Tuluk would have posted.

Tuluk smiled. He truly did enjoy this part of the game. He would have been a great sub-rosa espionage agent, he often thought.

The com unit on Cinch's beltline cheeped. Given that his com was on his pants and his pants were neatly hung on a hook against the gym's far wall, he had to amble that way to click the unit on—the voxcontrol was off-line, since he didn't want to be yelling at the com from across the room and maybe have somebody overhear him.

"Yeah?"

"Hey, old ranger. How you holding up?"

He grinned. "Not too bad, old pub owner."

"Listen, that thing we talked about, it's a done deal."

"Appreciate it."

"Why don't you drop by here in the morning and let's you and I roll around and break a little furniture?"

Cinch chuckled. If somebody had his com leeched, that ought to give them something to think about.

"Sounds good to me. See you about eight."

"Discom it," she said.

Cinch put his com on standby again and went back to the mag machine. At his age, you had to keep the blood circulating and the muscles flexing or time might get ahead of you. With Wanita, the blood circulated just fine. Sore as he was, the magnetic weights he had been moving made him feel better. He could still bench his own kiloage ten times, and while that didn't make him real strong, it kept him as strong as he'd ever been. A man had to do what he could.

As he punched in a weight, he smiled. There were reasons to stay in shape other than just to keep ahead of the bad guys.

"What?" Tuluk said.

Lobang came into the office, waved a small flatscreen. "The ranger and Wanita are playing dork and bush," he said. "Damn, that's hard to believe."

"Why, because she turned *you* down?"

"She didn't turn me down," Lobang said. "I never asked her."

Tuluk smiled. Perhaps he hadn't said it in so many words, but if he'd dropped any more broad hints in front of the black pubwoman, they'd be stacked so high they'd reach the ceiling. Must be quite a blow to Lobang's ego to have her pass on him and pick the less muscular, older—and thus much inferior in Lobang's eyes—ranger. Tuluk might not be the galaxy's greatest expert on women, if indeed the galaxy could claim to *have* an expert on women, but he knew that Lobang's swarthy good looks and big muscles wouldn't compensate for his tiny brain in the eyes of a fem like Wanita. She was too smart herself just to want a dick-in-the-box.

"Well, I never did," Lobang said.

"Lobang, do you think I care? Do you think anybody cares? It might be something we can use."

"They are getting together again in the morning." Lobang waved the flatscreen.

"Good. Maybe if he's busy having his lizard milked he won't be getting in our way."

Lobang shrugged, and Tuluk saw that the ranger's success with Wanita bothered him. Too bad. Lobang's ego seemed to be bigger than his biceps and that was *his* problem. There were times when keeping the big man around seemed to be a lot of trouble. One day it might get to be too much and he would have to go. Knowing what he knew, however, he couldn't be allowed to leave just like that. An accident would have to be arranged.

"Just keep your people on him," Tuluk said. "And don't say, 'You're the boss.' All right?"

Lobang opened his mouth, seemed for a moment like a fish gasping for water, then shut up without speaking.

As he left, Tuluk shook his head. Don't pee on the rug on your way out, he thought. Be a good doggy.

chapter 16

The shower felt good and he didn't spare the hot water or the foaming gel. He used the no-fog mirror to see his face while he depilated, to make sure he got all his whiskers. Didn't want any burry patches left. Never know when his face might be called on to rub something tender, and he didn't want to be using sandpaper. He smiled and ran his hands over his face. Smooth as a cue ball. Well. A cue ball with a few wrinkles and scars on it, anyhow.

As Cinch stepped out of the shower, his com chimed again.

"Yo?"

"M. Rudyard Carston? ID 436705369AF?"

"Yep, that's me."

"This is Pos Manusi at the GalaxNet office in Lembukota."

"What can I do for you, M. Manusi?"

"I have a sealed com from Stellar Ranger HQ for you, came in on the mail drophopper ten minutes ago."

"Thanks. I'll pick it up in the morning."

"Uh . . . it's marked 'Urgent,' Ranger."

Cinch had to smile at the unseen speaker. The message was, at the minimum, a week old. Likely older than that, given the vagaries of ship schedules in this quadrant. Probably had been sent before he arrived here and thus couldn't have anything to do with what he'd learned so

111

far. But civilians did get agitated when they saw official dispatches. "Thanks for your concern, but it'll keep until morning."

All clean and shiny, he padded naked to the bed and slid under the sheet. As he drifted to sleep, he rolled the ideas he'd been having around in his head. Could be things were maybe a little more complicated than he'd first thought. Well. If that was the case, he'd just have to unwind it all a bit more carefully, that was all. Hell, he was a Stellar Ranger, wasn't he? The complex stuff they ate for breakfast, right?

Right.

"My brother will be here in ten minutes," Wanita said, pulling the tabs on Cinch's shirt open. "Think you can manage something that fast?"

He laughed. "I'm not that old."

Afterward, as Cinch hustled into his clothes, he said, "Knowing that I'm being watched, isn't it risky for Pan to be sneaking in here?"

"Oh, he's been here for a couple of hours. He's down the hall in the spare room, reading or watching the entcom channel."

Cinch raised an eyebrow.

"Well, I needed this ten minutes. It's been so long for me, you know?"

"Yesterday was that long ago?"

"Eons, Ranger."

They both smiled.

Cinch followed Wanita into the pub itself, not yet open for business. After a couple of minutes, Pan came in. He was grinning.

"Something funny, little brother?"

He made a show of sniffing the air. "Smells funny in here," he said. "Smells like . . . oh, hmm . . . what *is* that smell?"

"Fuck off, Pan."

"Too late," he said, "you beat me to it, at least according to my nose."

Cinch watched them as he listened to the banter. These two liked each other.

"So, what can a bandito do for the Stellar Rangers?"

Cinch had already decided he was going to trust Wanita, and by extension, Pan. They might be part of a conspiracy, but he didn't believe it. You got to know somebody a little when you screwed your brains out with her, and it was not logical but it worked for Cinch.

"Our friend Tuluk is up to something," Cinch said. "Something highly illegal he doesn't want anybody to know about."

"You mean out in the blueweed patch?"

Cinch leaned back against the bar and looked at Pan with a sharper eye. "You ahead of me here?"

Pan shrugged. He did look a lot like his sister. "Not really. He's touchy about everything, but seems to get particularly upset if we poke a finger in that direction. I thought at first it might be the blueweed itself, but that doesn't make any sense. No way to steal the stuff and boil it down unless you can run trucks and build a major processing lab, and he knows the raj can't do either."

"Any ideas as to what it might be?"

Pan shook his head. "Could be anything. Maybe he's cooking and eating people out there. Sacrificing them to his patron demon. No way to tell."

"I think there might be a way," Cinch said. "But I'll need your help to do it."

"Call it. You got it."

Tuluk glanced at the chrono inset in the limo's backseat for the eighth or ninth time. Ulang was late. It was half an hour past midnight and there was no sign of them. He leaned forward.

In the front seat, Lobang anticipated the question and said, "No sign on the radar, boss. Maybe he ain't coming."

Tuluk leaned back. "He's coming. He's just very cautious. In his business, mistakes are very expensive and sometimes fatal."

Outside, the night had chilled, like a bottle of champagne buried in ice. The sky was crystal and thick with stars, the air still as the inside of a casket. From where the limo was parked on the mesa, Tuluk could see the ground below for a hundred klicks in all directions. It was mostly bare, save for scrub growth and rocks, sand and dirt; if the lizards or night birds were about, they padded or flew silently. Tuluk had the window down and the frosty air ghosted into the vehicle with invisible tentacles, touching his face softly.

"Good evening, M. Tuluk," a voice said.

Tuluk jumped, nearly hit his head on the limo's roof. Lobang swiveled in the driver's seat and came around with his handgun drawn.

Outside the car stood Ulang the dope merchant.

"Good God, man, how did you get here?"

Ulang was tall, thin to the point of emaciation, with excellent teeth and a shock of red hair even the dark couldn't disguise. He said, "Tell your muscle to put his weapon away."

Tuluk waved at Lobang and the gun disappeared.

"If I may . . . ?"

Tuluk slid over and Ulang opened the limo's door and got in.

"Cold out there," he said. Given that he wore expensive heat threads with gloves and a headband, Tuluk doubted that he much felt the night's chill.

"How did you—?"

"It's a big part of my business to be careful, M. Tuluk, and how I go about it is something I prefer to keep secret. I am wanted on several planets, and some of the rewards are quite substantial."

"I understand. Though you are taking a big risk for all your stealth. What if Lobang and I were Intergalactic Drug Enforcement agents?"

Ulang smiled. "Iggy? You?"

Although it was as remote a possibility as being able to breathe water or fly by wiggling his toes, it irritated Tuluk that Ulang dismissed it so easily. He did not like being irritated by one such as Ulang.

"Why not? As you said, the rewards are quite high."

Ulang's thin face lost its humor and grew hard. "The

sum of all the rewards out for my capture would not equal a week's income for you."

"Still, it is an interesting thought. If we were Iggy, we would have you."

Ulang's humor returned. He chuckled. "So you would. Except for this." He pulled a small electronic control from his pocket. "I have a two-meter length of pyrohex cord wrapped around my waist, with a primer tuned to a complicated frequency," he said. "If I raise the protector, like so, and press this button, guess what will happen?"

In the front seat, Lobang sucked in a quick breath.

Ulang's smile grew. "Your muscle knows what pyrohex is, I see."

"Lobang?"

"Yessir. It's military-grade shape-charge explosive. If he's got two meters of it on him and it goes off, all that will be left of us and the car will be a crater deep enough you could use it for a swimming pool. Deep enough you could use a diving board at the end and not hit your head on the bottom."

Tuluk nodded, unafraid. He preferred dealing with careful men.

"Very good, M. Ulang. I like your style. Shall we get down to business?"

Ulang stared at him for a moment. Tuluk fancied that the merchant saw the lack of fear in him and when he did, he put the control away. "Let's do that."

Cinch took the message tube from the clerk at the postal net office. It was a bucky-metal one-time, looked much like a solid gray gelcap rounded on both ends, about the size of a child's forearm. In theory, if anybody tried to open it without using the addressee's personal security code, the entire capsule would disintegrate, taking with it the chemically treated plastic of the info-marble inside. Codes could be cracked, of course, but even so the tube wouldn't reseal. In theory.

Outside in the already warm and dry day, Cinch popped the seal using his code and rolled the info-marble out into his palm. He pulled his reader from his belt, clicked the ball into place, and put the short-range L-O-S plug into his left ear for privacy. He lit the reading laser and played the vox-only message. It was a one-timer too, so he listened carefully as the voice of Sector Commander Ingmar "Hacksaw" Harvey came to faux-life in his ear:

"Hello, Cinch, and I hope you are enjoying your stay on lovely Roget. I was there once, thirty years or so ago, and unless it's changed radically, it's hot, dry and boring."

Well, Cinch thought, two out of three. But then he was seldom if ever bored, no matter where he was. Being bored, Cinch figured, was the mark of a less than mature mind.

"Probably nothing I can say at this remove is gonna do you much good, but there's a couple things you ought to know FYI.

"First, we started getting heat about sending a ranger to yon backrocket planet before your ship got fifteen minutes into the Warp. Somebody's got a big ear and they got the word to somebody with a bigger mouth real quick. Assume, if you haven't already, that every move you make is watched by unfriendly eyes."

Cinch had to grin. Every ranger always assumed that on every assignment, if he or she wanted to live to retire. Or just until the case was over. But Hacksaw always reminded them. He was like a mama dog with puppies sometimes.

"Second thing is, we've come across some intelligence that suggests something is brewing over and above the original complaints we got. Something of a major nature. Now I don't have anything specific to give you on this, but every time the name 'Roget' comes up in certain circles, expressions get blank or eyebrows get raised and ice wouldn't melt on normally hot foreheads, if you get my drift."

Cinch nodded at the recorded voice of a man who was light-years away. The key term here was "certain circles." In ranger parlance, that meant other agencies who fielded their own peace, or control officers. That covered a lot of territory, of course: G-marsh, Delivery Service Operations, Galactic Security, the Intergalactic Drug Enforcement Agency, IG Monetary Patrol, plus half a dozen smaller operations—not to mention the tens of thousands of system or local police departments. It could mean something. *What* could be almost anything. There was a lot of petty crap that went on between those in charge of enforcing various aspects of the law and sharing information was not high on anybody's list. On a good day you might get rangers to trust other rangers—getting them to trust a Gooney, Dipso, Iggy or Coinflipper was impossible. Cinch didn't feel too bad about the derogatory nicknames for the other operatives on the galactic level, given that they called rangers Shit Stompers—though not to their faces if they wanted to keep low premiums on their dental insurance.

"Anyway, kid, that's the news from home. What I hope is, you've already gotten this sucker cleared and are on a ship heading home, but if not, watch your ass. Something's off there and you don't want to get caught flat-footed. That's a discom. Later."

Cinch pulled the earplug and tucked it back into the reader, then ejected the ball. Nothing there worth worrying about, and the ball was supposed to be wiped, but he would drop it in a disposal grinder somewhere to be sure.

Hmm. Interesting that somebody offworld had figured out what he had, that there was more than met the eye on first look here. 'Course that also meant he might be running into more trouble and that wasn't good. Ah, well. If the job was easy, anybody could do it.

He grinned and walked across the dusty road toward Wanita's. It had its compensations, the job.

chapter 17

"This whole thing is as illegal as hell," Pan said. "I thought you were a lawman, a peace officer." But he grinned.

Cinch nodded. "Yep, it is illegal, technically speaking. And there are worlds where it would be cause for serious character revision and a long stay in locktime. But out here on the frontier, you have to work with what you have. If I'm wrong, I'll pay the Devil. Sometimes the end justifies the means. Not always. Whether it does here or not, we'll just have to see."

Wanita laughed behind them as she charged the drink dispenser with carbonation. "Well, well. Listen to the police officer and the bandit discussing the philosophy of crime."

"I don't think you're wrong," Pan said. "But then, I'm biased. If you told me Manis Tuluk ate babies for breakfast, I'd believe it."

"I doubt there's any profit in such a diet. I think that's what drives Tuluk, profit. Old ranger investigative techniques say if you can find out where the bad guys get their money, you can usually solve the crime. My guess is that whatever Tuluk is doing in the blueweed, it's designed to generate income."

Wanita said, "You'd think he has enough money—he's got more than anybody else on the planet."

"But he doesn't have more than anybody in the galaxy. With really rich people, money is not so important in itself, it is more how they keep score. Get the most, you win."

"Crazy," Pan said.

"May be, but that's not our problem. How is your end of things shaping up?"

"No problem. Diji and Po are off in Cube City buying the supplies you wanted. I don't suppose you'll let us keep any leftovers after we're done?"

"If my suspicions about Tuluk prove out, you won't need them. You might start thinking about how to make an honest living, Pan."

The young man smiled. "Why would I want to do that? I'll just wait for my sister to croak and take over the pub."

"Given the way you behave, little brother, I'll outlive you by fifty years."

"Ah, well."

"How about the rest of it?" Cinch asked.

"Abrikos and Darah are scouting for the best location. Bedil is, ah . . . arranging our transportation."

Cinch smiled at the euphemism for stealing a van and a flitter.

"That's about it."

Cinch nodded again. "Okay. The weathercast says there is a front moving this way, due here tomorrow night. Could produce fog, rain, maybe some hail. Unless you know of any reason not to, we'll do it then."

"Sooner the better," Pan said. "We'll be ready."

Darkness lay thickly over the blueweed field, night having spent half her allotted time creating the starry ebon cloak.

"What is this guy, a vampire?" Lobang said. "He only comes out at night and when he does, he's smoke or a bat or something?"

Tuluk smiled. Now and again, Lobang would turn a phrase or make a suggestion that showed he wasn't completely without wit. On the one hand, it was all too rare a break; on the other hand, you did not want somebody *too* bright standing behind you.

Tuluk leaned back against the wall of the shed and said, "What he is is an intergalactic merchant who deals in illegal recreation chemicals. While I personally have never believed it is any of a government's business what you do to your own body as long as you don't inflict it on anybody else, our man Ulang has broken so many laws on so many planets that he couldn't serve all the accumulated time if he had a dozen lifespans at his beck."

"Yeah, well, I've got the doppler cranked up high and perimeter sensors ringing this place. He won't sneak up on us this time."

"The rain will ruin the sensors, won't it?"

"I'll pull them before it starts to rain. Right now, I want eyes. I don't want him waltzing in on us like before."

As indeed he did not; a blip on Lobang's detection gear indicated the approach of a low-flying craft, skimming along at almost weedtop level, coming in fast from the northwest.

"Ah. Our guest has arrived. You do have your men in place?"

"They're out there. If that flitter doesn't flash the right code in the next thirty seconds, the boys are gonna open up on it with their 15mm recoilless rifles and it's gonna be smoking history."

But the silent and coded signal must have be delivered by the pulse-radio onboard the vessel, for the night air remained quiet, unshattered by automatic gunfire.

After a few moments, the flitter came into sight, sans running lights, and settled into the landing area close to the shack. Tuluk and Lobang walked toward it, the larger man keeping one hand near his pistol as they did so.

"Evening," Ulang said, as he alighted from his vehicle. "My compliments on your security. I assume the six men you have hidden in the crop are carrying weaponry capable of downing a flitter like this one?"

"Yeah, they are," Lobang said, obviously irritated that Ulang had spotted his troops.

"Good. Then we won't be bothered by somebody dropping in unexpectedly."

"No," Tuluk said.

"Not that I expect there's anybody on your planet who'd be likely to do that anyhow—except for one man."

Tuluk kept his face as blank as he could. How the hell could he know about the ranger?

"You didn't mention him when we spoke earlier," Ulang said. "The ranger, I mean."

"It wasn't necessary. He's no threat. We have him under surveillance at all times."

"M. Tuluk, having some experience in these matters, let me tell you that a Stellar Ranger is *always* a threat."

Cinch sat up in the bed and pivoted, put his feet on the floor.

"Where are you going?" Wanita said. Sleep fogged her voice.

"To the fresher. Then I need to get dressed and head back to Kohl's."

"Why? Somebody expecting you? Somebody young and beautiful, maybe?"

Cinch chuckled. "Whatever she expects, she isn't going to get it."

"Then why go? Stay here. Let me wake up in the morning and feed you breakfast. I like having you sleep next to me."

Cinch thought about it. Why not? He was a big boy, Kohl didn't keep tabs on him. And even if he had *wanted* to play games with Baji—which he did not—he wasn't going to be able to do it tonight, not after what Wanita had just done to him.

"You sure?"

"Yeah, old ranger, I'm sure."

"Okay. You twisted my arm."

"Was that what that was? Kinda small for an arm."

"It gets bigger. Under the right circumstances."

"Brag, brag. You're all alike, you men."

He laughed, and went to use the fresher.

* * *

Ulang was impressed, Tuluk could tell, even though he affected otherwise. The operation wasn't much to look at, but the numbers were enough to make even a wealthy man think.

"My scientist's projections indicate we can expect half to three-quarters of the current test crop to be psychoactive."

"Which means, in terms of finished product . . . ?"

"Around three hundred thousand doses, give or take."

Tuluk could almost hear the man's mental gears whirring. Three hundred thousand doses. His wholesale cost, what he would have to pay Tuluk, was somewhere around eighty-five MU a dose, that would work out to more than twenty-five million. He could turn that around for almost twice the price in the trade lanes, so he would net about the same. What the suckers paid for it at the retail end might be two, two-fifty a pop, so it wasn't a poor man's chem, but there would be no shortage of buyers. While twenty-five million was not a major fortune, it wasn't something to spit on, either. But this was just a *test* crop.

"I'll have ten times that much blueweed converted to the Twist within three or four seasons," Tuluk said. Now *there* was a major fortune. Five or six years would make both of them multibillionaires. With that kind of wealth, Tuluk could pyramid himself up to a galactic shaker. Since big money was like gravity, the more of it you had, the more you could attract. Only a handful of players had ten billion to work with.

"Jesus and Buddha," Ulang said. Now his voice was full of undisguised awe.

"Indeed. So, M. Ulang, are we in business?"

Ulang managed a smile. "Oh, I would say so, M. Tuluk. I think you and I are going to make each other very, very happy."

Morning seeped into Wanita's bedroom, followed by a less than quiet tapping on the door.

"What?" Wanita said.

"If you and your boyfriend can untangle yourselves, he

and I have serious business to take care of," Pan yelled through the door.

Cinch, snuggled against Wanita's backside, was not the least bit interested in moving.

"What makes you think he's in here?"

"Come on, big sister, our mother didn't raise any foolish children. Or deaf ones, either. I heard you two half the night. Cinch? Are your intentions toward my sister honorable?"

Cinch chuckled. "As honorable as rangers can get, yes."

"It's a good thing. Well, I'll be waiting in the pub. People your age ought to be ashamed of yourselves, behaving that way!" He padded away down the hall.

Wanita rolled over to face Cinch. "Hi, soldier. New in town?"

"I'd better get dressed."

"My little brother needs to learn patience. Let him wait."

She giggled and reached for him.

It was half an hour before Cinch made it to the pub, where Pan had the microwave cooker frying steaks and what passed for potatoes on this world. The smell was thick and appetizing.

"You'd like your meat medium rare?"

"Close enough."

Pan nodded. "She really likes you, you know."

"It's mutual."

"It's been three or four years since she was with anybody. Treat her well, okay?"

"Best I can. What's up?"

"Diji and Po are back, we've got the places picked out, I've got the map here." He waved an infoball. "We're ready if you are."

Cinch nodded. "Tonight it is, then."

"I hope you're right about this. But if not, what the hell—it'll be worth it anyhow."

"It's a risk, Pan. I don't want anybody getting killed.

Wanita would be real unhappy if she had to scatter your ashes."

"Don't worry about me. We're sons of the desert, the raj, we move like ghosts, we fade into the shadows. You take care of your part, we'll do ours."

Cinch nodded. "I think those steaks must be about ready."

"Maybe I'll get a job as a cook," Pan said.

"Maybe you should apply to the Stellar Ranger Academy."

Pan laughed. "Right."

Cinch put one of the steaks on the platter, but didn't speak.

"You serious?"

"You're young, strong, not too bright, you'd fit right in."

"With my record?"

"Admissions gives a lot of weight to field recs. I could put in a word for you." He sawed a piece of the meat off and popped it into his mouth. He chewed the bite. Bland, it needed seasoning. He looked around for condiments.

Pan appeared stunned, or at least shaken. Cinch smiled inwardly, keeping his face neutral.

"You'd do that for me?"

"Sure. Why not? I get a couple more suckers enrolled, my curse is lifted and they let me go."

"Outside of Wanita and the raj, nobody has ever cared much what happened to me. Thanks, Cinch. I appreciate it."

"Well, given the steak, you won't do real well as a cook."

Both men were smiling when Wanita arrived. She looked at them both carefully.

"What did I miss?"

"Your boyfriend is trying to get me a job."

"That would be a miracle."

"Yeah, especially the job he's talking about. Tell me, do I look like ranger material?"

"Actually, you look more like rootsacking material."

"Thank you so much, sister dearest. You want a steak?"

"Not if *you* cooked it."

Cinch laughed.

chapter 18

"Where were you last night?"

Cinch looked at Baji and now he did feel more like her father than potential lover. "Excuse me?"

"You didn't come back to the ranch, you must have stayed *some*where."

Cinch had returned to pack his gear and to let Kohl know he was still alive, as well as to set up his little caper. He'd been on his way to the man's study when Baji stopped him in the hall outside his bedroom. She stood looking up at him from a meter and a half away, waiting for his answer. She wore a thin yellow silk bathrobe belted shut at the waist but gaping everywhere else and, as far as he could tell, nothing under it. Odd how detached he was about that bare flesh now. Almost amazing, actually.

He gave her the most innocuous reply he could. "Yes. I stayed somewhere."

"Where?"

Cinch took deep breath. She wasn't going to let it go and he didn't have time to play long games with her today. Okay, he would give it a quick try, to be easy on her. He said, "Listen, Baji, you're a nice girl—"

She scrunched her face up, mouth tight, eyes narrowed. She crossed her arms and tried to wither him with her glare. "You slept with that slut Wanita, didn't you? Don't bother to deny it because I know it's true!"

126

"Yes, I was with Wanita. But—"

"What? What? Don't say you're sorry, I'm not going to forgive you just like that!"

"I'm not sorry. And it's not any of your business what I do or who I do it with."

He thought for a moment she might explode, figuratively, at least. When she spoke, it was an angry rush of disbelief, an acidic spew, the volume going up with each breath: "You fucked that *whore* when you could have had *me?* I'm younger and prettier and richer and smarter and there's nothing *she* can do that *I* can't do! I've been with men, I know what men want!" This last was a flat-out yell.

Well, shit. Not any way around it now.

"Wanita is an adult, just like I am an adult. We're both older than your father. You're still a young woman—"

"But I'm not a little girl!" She stamped her foot.

"You're acting like one. Like a child who hasn't figured out that she can't always get what she wants."

She was white with rage now. "You wanted *me* before! You wanted me a lot! I know, I could tell! You aren't so damned smart, you aren't! We'll see who gets what they want! We'll see! You'll be sorry! You *will* be sorry!"

She spun and marched away, trying to look haughty he guessed, but only managing a series of stiff, puppetlike bounces. If she wasn't so upset, he would have laughed at how cute she looked. Kind of like a kitten pretending she'd lost interest in a ball of string.

An *old* ball of string . . .

Behind him, Kohl cleared his throat.

Cinch turned around.

"Sorry. Probably they could hear her in town. I can't say you handled that real well, son, even if it's all true."

"I don't know what else I could have said. I chose to spend my time with Wanita instead of Baji. No way I can dress it up so it's anything but a rejection. I get the feeling she doesn't have to deal with that much."

Kohl shook his head. "No, she doesn't have to deal with it much. Hardly ever. That's my fault as much as it is hers. I look at her, and I see my life when I was young and stupid. I wanted it to be easier for her than it was for me."

"You turned out okay. If the fire doesn't cook you, it tempers you. She needs to know what heat feels like, otherwise she'll hurt people because she doesn't know what it means to *get* hurt."

"Easy for you to say, you'll be pulling out when this is over. I have to live with her after you've gone." But he smiled to show he understood and didn't begrudge Cinch for what he'd said. "Well. I suppose she'd have to deal with it sooner or later. Better while she's young enough to heal quick from it."

"I'll be out again tonight."

Kohl raised an eyebrow.

"Not to town. Attending to . . . ranger business. But if I don't show up in a couple-three days, you might want to pass this along to the Stellar Ranger Sector HQ." He handed the older man a sealed message tube. In it was an outline, along with his notes and suspicions about Tuluk, all recorded on a hardcast infoball. Hacksaw would know what to do if it showed up, and what that meant.

"You expecting to run into trouble?"

"You can't say no."

"You need any help? I can field a few good hands."

"Thanks, Gus, but I can handle it. More people wouldn't do any good."

"All right. Take care, then, son."

"Thanks, Gus. Hope to see you in a couple of days. I'm sorry about Baji."

"It couldn't be helped. I appreciate you not making it worse by sleeping with her."

Cinch left the older man standing there holding the message tube and went to start his caper.

Tuluk couldn't really be said to be entertaining his guest, but he did in fact have the drug merchant at his ranch. They sat at the long tulipwood table in the formal dining room, enjoying a meal his chef had labored over most of the day.

Ulang sliced a small chunk of meat from steak and chewed it. Here was a man who had, despite his thinness, indulged himself in good food a time or two. He closed his eyes and savored the flavor, a small smile shining. After he swallowed, he said, "Excellent. What kind of meat?"

"Infant ularsinga. A type of local lizard."

Ulang nodded, cut another sliver of the steak, put it into his mouth.

"The adults grow to a rather formidable size," Tuluk said, slicing at his own. "The only way to get the babies is to kill the watch parent. One of them stays with the pups while the other forages, until the young are old enough to hunt on their own. Once they reach that age, the meat becomes too gamy."

Ulang chewed thoughtfully. "Expensive, I bet. Does it dry freeze for travel?"

Tuluk smiled. "It isn't actually for sale commercially, at least not in any quantity. Runs maybe three hundred a half-kilo, if you can find a local rancher who will sell it. But I'd be happy to have the cook block up a few kilos for you to take when you leave."

"You are too kind."

"Not at all. The least I can do for a new partner. Care for a little more wine? It's *biru buah anggur,* made from blue grapes grown in the Bintang Sector."

"I believe I will have another glass. It, too, is excellent," Ulang said. "It complements the meat perfectly."

Before he finished speaking, the waiter arrived with the wine bottle and poured a generous amount into his half-empty crystal stemware. The wine cost more than the baby ularsinga would.

"You are obviously a man of discriminating tastes," Tuluk said, snipping at his own wine. Even if he was a dope seller, it was interesting to have a gourmet at his table, given that most of the staff were happy to wash down green beef jerky with local beer, belching all the way. One had to take one's appreciative audience where one could find it, Tuluk supposed.

"Perhaps after dinner we might enjoy cigars and some single-malt scotch or brandy while we discuss the details of our new venture?"

"M. Tuluk—"

"Call me 'Manis.' "

Ulang grinned. "You are a man after my own heart, Manis."

The team following Cinch during the day usually numbered five, as best he could tell, each in his or her own vehicle and working carefully so that none of them was ever in his line of sight too long before being replaced by another. They were competent, but he had followed enough subjects that it hadn't taken him long to spot them. The SOP was to pretend you didn't see them, so they wouldn't know they were burned; otherwise, they would be replaced and you had to ferret them out again. Better the devils you knew than the ones you didn't.

At night, however, the tail was shortened and shrunk. Only two operatives kept watch on him. Assuming he would have to sleep some time and having demonstrated his preference for that after dark, they felt they could afford to be lax.

Cinch, now dressed in his camo gear, slipped from one of the house's side windows and moved into the night. Because they couldn't get too close to Kohl's ranch house proper, the pair of agents were hidden in carefully excavated ground blinds, one in front and one in back, with, he assumed, decent optical equipment trained on the house's entrances. Probably the scopes were rigged with motion detectors so that if the doors opened, an alarm would wake a dozing operative in time to get a quick look at who caused it before they got very far. With a sixth- or seventh-generation LG eye lit and working, they would be able to see the exits under available starlight as if it were noon—albeit a somewhat cloudy and green-tinted noon.

But as Cinch half-crawled, half-duckwalked away from the building and toward the garage, he smiled at how easy it was to slip surveillance in this kind of setup. The scopes and electronics would probably be top quality, but at the range the watchers were from the house they would necessarily have a very tight field of view. From a kilometer away you could certainly see a man open a door but without magnification, you wouldn't be able to tell who he might be. Even a power zoom wasn't instantaneous; so while you could rig your scope relatively wide to see the entire door and area around it, a much bigger field wouldn't give you the detail you needed. And if the damned electronics fizzled, as they sometimes did at just the wrong time, you would have to manually refield and you might well miss your subject in the dark, he was in a hurry. So watching the whole house was not impossible, but real unlikely, which meant nobody was going to see him leave via the window because nobody expected that and so wouldn't be set up to cover it.

Cinch reached the garage and slipped in through the door he'd left open earlier. Inside was a bike he'd set up, with a nearly silent fuel-cell electric motor connected to the rear wheel. It wasn't fast but it was quiet, and he had a relatively smooth route picked out that angled away from the two watchers. As long as there wasn't a third one he'd missed, he would be a dozen klicks away in half an hour and the two in the blinds would not suspect a thing.

He rolled the bike out on the dark side of the garage and switched on the motor. He climbed onto the bike and engaged the drive. He and the little bike moved off.

The watchers had similar vehicles hidden in their lairs, but if they suspected he was gone, it was their coms they would use, not their wheels. He couldn't outrun a radio pulse, so the trick lay in keeping quiet and not being seen.

And, as the bike jumped across the unpaved ground, keeping himself from being tossed off by a bad bump and breaking his neck was also a consideration. . . .

Pan had his borrowed truck parked ten kilometers away, under the overhang of a rocky outcropping on a smallish hill, with camouflage netting strung over the exposed side. If Cinch hadn't known it was there, he would have missed the van.

Cinch whistled as he drew near, loudly, a five-note sequence he and Pan had agreed on. He kept the bike's lights off as he rolled up to the netting.

"Evening, Ranger. Nice night for a ride."

Actually it was nicer than Cinch had hoped. The promised weather front had stalled, and while there were a few high clouds, there wasn't any fog or rain apparent in the near future.

"Any trouble?" Pan said.

"Nope. You set?"

"Yep. Want to take a look at your new ride?"

Cinch followed Pan around the end of the netting. The younger man opened the back of the van. Inside, Diji and Po sat, playing cards on a box between them. They nodded at Cinch, made polite and somewhat nervous noises at him.

"There it is," Pan said, pointing.

Cinch looked at the small vehicle. It was a two-passenger flitter, looking much like a motorcycle without wheels, with a black plastic faring and clear windshield and a big repellor unit amidships. "Very nice," he said. "A racing model."

"Yeah, and take good care of it," Po said. "We couldn't find what you wanted on the street so I borrowed this from my uncle. You wreck it and he will skin me with a bent gravy spoon."

Cinch smiled. "I'll be careful."

Pan blew out a nervous breath.

"You okay?"

The young man nodded. "Yeah. A little tense."

"That's okay, so am I."

"You?"

"Risking your life is something you only get used to in the abstract," Cinch said. "When it gets to the actual event, the pucker-factor still happens every time."

"Pucker-factor?"

Cinch grinned. "How tight your anal sphincter gets in response to danger. On a scale from one to ten, one is hardly noticeable, ten is so strong it would suck up a couch if you were sitting on it."

Pan and his two friends laughed.

"So, let's get this bird into the air, okay?" Cinch said. "Before my PF gets too high to let me use the seat."

"Right."

The four of them moved the flitter out of van and down the ramp extruded from the rear. When it was on the ground, Cinch powered up the vehicle's computer and downloaded the map from his flatscreen into the navigation program. He checked to make sure it was glitch-free, ran a quick diagnostic on the flitter's systems, then nodded. "Looks good. Let's make sure our chronographs are in tune."

The four checked and adjusted their personal timers so they all matched.

"Let's do it," Cinch said.

He climbed onto the flitter, fixed the seat, powered the repellor up. The machine hummed quietly to life.

"Good luck," Cinch said.

"You, too," Pan responded.

With that, the ranger sped off into the night.

chapter **19**

Even at half throttle, the little flitter was fast. Cinch rocketed over the mostly barren ground at just over two hundred kilometers an hour, maintaining a height that would have clipped the tops of short trees, had there been any. It wouldn't fool a good simadam running doppler, but ground clutter ought to cause regular radar problems spotting him. What he hoped was, anybody normally looking for him would be too busy by the time he got there.

Crouched down low behind the windshield, Cinch swung a long and wide turn to the northwest, circling around Tuluk's property. His destination was logged into the navicomp and the flitter could take him there on its own, but he preferred to keep manual control. If something happened to him before he got there, the map program he'd loaded was rigged to erase itself so nobody would ever be sure where he'd been going, at least nobody who shouldn't know.

The night air was crisp, and blowing past at two hundred per, bit at any part of him that was exposed. He'd raised his head above the shield once, and his hair had streamed as the wind took his breath and watered his eyes. He'd quickly ducked back behind the protection. A fat night bug would be an organic bullet at this speed, could put out an eye or maybe even knock him senseless. He should have gotten a helmet to go with the eyewear; that would have been smart, too.

Ah, well. So he wouldn't win any prizes for brainpower. He could live with it.

Time passed, and Cinch monitored its passage. That part was critical. Too soon, and there was a chance some doo-dah with a spookscope might see and shoot him out of the air; too late, and the same thing applied. He'd be dead and that was bad. He'd never know what exactly old Tuluk had been up to, and somehow that was almost worse. Solving the puzzle was what kept a ranger sharp, what kept him going.

He grinned and opened the flitter's throttle a little more. The night world blurred past. He still believed that when your number came due, you paid the price; but he had begun to realize that since you didn't know when it was about to appear on the horizon, there wasn't any point in being *too* fatalistic. You took that to the extreme and you could justify jumping off a tall building into the plastcrete.

Tuluk and Ulang were considering the details of delivery, how best to distance themselves from the freighters that would be hauling the refined chem. Tuluk was willing to defer to Ulang's experience in these matters, but he wanted to know the particulars. Knowledge was indeed power, and he preferred to keep as much of that for himself as possible. As always, forewarned was forearmed.

"I always use a ship of Gowah or Gorn registry whenever possible," Ulang was saying. "They are both particularly paranoid about secrecy, which is how they keep offworld moneys coming into their treasury—"

The door to the study zipped open and Lobang ran into the room.

"What are you doing?"

"Sorry, boss, but we got trouble. The pipeline—"

"Send the leak patrol. I'm busy here."

"Uh, boss, it ain't just a leak. Somebody blew it the fuck up. In a bunch of places."

Tuluk stared at Lobang as if he had just sprouted quills. Blew it up?

Dammit!

Cinch glanced at his chrono. If everything had gone as planned, the raj had just set off a bunch of explosive charges, shattering the pipeline that fed Tuluk's blueweed fields. The system had been designed to stop major leaks. Automatic valves were set to kick in way up the line if the flow increased past a certain point. All that valuable water wasn't supposed to be feeding desert scrub, and any halfwit computer watch program would know that. But the automatic valves had been given other instructions, courtesy of the raj. Somebody was going to have to turn a shutoff manually, and some of those had been tampered with, too.

As if somebody *wanted* to waste all Tuluk's water. Imagine that.

It wouldn't take all that much to stop the flow, despite the sabotage. The computer would find a good valve and somebody would get sent to it in a few minutes, fifteen, twenty, no more. Rebuilding the shattered line would only take a few days, if that. No, it wasn't a big disaster, but it was big enough for an anxious man to scramble his troops to see what was going on. Especially since the raj would continue setting off more fireworks designed to draw as much attention as possible.

With any luck, Tuluk would think there was a full-blown war cranking up out in the northeastern badlands and he'd have to take appropriate action.

And while he was over there, Cinch would be over *here*.

He was on-line now, skimming the tops of the tallest blueweed plants. He couldn't assume that Tuluk would leave the shed completely unattended, not if what was there was as valuable as a springdog guard would indicate. And he had to consider the biomech, too. It might be back on-line. Armor-piercing didn't work all that well at hand-gun velocities, but he had his carbine loaded for electronic and plated bear. If they sicced a dog on him again, they were going to be out more of their expensive hardware.

He also couldn't expect to fly up to the door and stroll in. He would have to put the flitter down far enough away so the sound wouldn't reach his target, and so any detection systems that might be up and running wouldn't get a good look at him before he vanished.

Tricky.

He decided to drop the flitter into a lane between rows and baby it along to within a kilometer or so before he started walking. He could jog the remaining distance in a few minutes and still be in and out before Tuluk's troops got through chasing after the raj. Who ought to be fanning away from the pipeline at a good clip by now.

The flitter chugged along, quiet but not silent; after the fast run through the night it felt as if he were crawling, even though he was still doing fifty.

Close enough.

He dropped the flitter almost to the ground, eased it into the weed out of sight, set his locater so he could find it if he got turned around.

Cinch took a deep breath, let it out. Time to take care of business.

"Christo, what a mess," Lobang said.

Looking down on the scene from fifty meters up in the limo, Tuluk agreed. The car's spotlights, dialed to broadbeam, revealed a section of the plastic pipeline. Or what had been a section of it; the explosives had shattered a good twenty meters of pipe into fragments, the largest of which seemed to be no bigger than a man's hand.

Ulang had elected to stay at the ranch and indicated that he might not be there when Tuluk returned. Chem peddlers were by nature cautious, even to the point of paranoia; and Ulang's first reaction had been to wonder if this debacle had been aimed at him.

"Take us to the next one," Tuluk said.

Lobang accelerated the limo. Four sections, hundreds of thousands if not millions of liters of water wasted. Lobang had a dozen men at each location running around waving guns, but they were a waste of time, Tuluk knew.

"We are going to have to do something about the raj," Tuluk said, his voice cold.

"You think this was them?"

"It's got their prints all over it. I want you to triple the offer of a reward on Panjang Meritja, same for his gang. Put it onto the net right away."

"We'll have bounty hunters crawling all over this place like ants on a dead mouse, boss."

"Good. Maybe if Pan knows he'll get his face shot off if he shows it, it'll give him something else to think about instead of aggravating me."

"Okay."

Tuluk leaned back in the plush seat and considered this most recent attack. What was to be gained here? Pan wasn't a stupid boy, at least not in terms of pure brain-power. He would have to know that bombing the pipeline would be a temporary irritation at best. He must have spent considerable resources setting this up: the cost of the explosives, the transportation, the planning. What was the point? There was nothing to be gained here, save to pull on his enemy's tail. It was not like breaking into a ware-house and stealing something of value. A couple of days and the line would be as good as new. So why would he make this gesture?

Probably the same reason he made all the other ges-tures. It was the best he could do, like a fly biting an el-ephant.

"Here's the second one," Lobang said.

Tuluk leaned his head out of the window. The air was frosty, his ears started to ache. Another big section of pipe had been pulverized. That would have taken a number of charges, placed sequentially—

Came the dawn of realization, all in a rush. "Oh, shit!"

"Boss?"

"It's a diversion! This isn't about the damned pipeline!"

"Huh?"

"The ranger, the goddamned ranger is sleeping with Wanita Meritja! He's using her to contact her brother! The *ranger* sent them to do this!"

"But—why?"

"The blueweed processing station. The Twist! He knows about it! Get on the com and call Picobe!"

Cinch looked and listened for the springdog, but so far hadn't detected it. He wore his wolf ears and spookeyes now and moved through the darkness easily, able to see almost as well as if it were daylight, able to hear much better than normally. This kind of augmentation was effective, but risky. If you got dependent on it and your electronics went wonky, you could find yourself in deep shit in a hurry.

But for the moment, moving toward the dimly lit shack just ahead, the extrasensory gear was a big help.

There was a generator thrumming along a few meters behind the main shed, under a low-roofed outbuilding that was basically four slabs of Everlast—a slant roof and three walls. Cinch guessed that this far out there weren't power lines laid and the city cast wouldn't reach, so the generator probably supplied all the power for the blueweed shed.

He edged his way toward the outbuilding. Still no sign of guards or the dog. He shut his wolf ears off. The generator would deafen him otherwise, it was loud enough to hurt but not so loud as to trip the safety cutout. He also slipped the spookeyes up on his forehead to examine the machinery up close.

The generator, a simple exchange-drive with a line going into the ground deep enough to tap into geothermal, was locked and needed a mechanical key to operate the controls. Cinch leaned his carbine against the wall of the shed and pulled a popper from his pouch. He set the popper—a melter rather than an explosive—just over the generator's drive shaft and triggered it. He looked away from the intensely bright light that resulted as the popper flared. Jesus, it lit the place up like noon! Hard shadows danced on the back of the nearby shed, and the stink of melting metal and plastic came forth in a boiling cloud of blue smoke.

Cinch grabbed his carbine and circled around behind the shed while the popper continued its work. The drive shaft was too hard to be affected by this relatively low heat device, but the casing around it was vulnerable.

A minute later the melting material must have started dripping. The generator's circuit breaker clicked and the unit's high whine dropped to a groan, then a growl as it shut down. The shed went dark.

Cinch slipped his wolfears on in time to hear a voice from inside the shed: "—fucker! What the hell happened?"

A second voice said, "Obviously the power source has malfunctioned."

"But we had a call coming in from the boss."

"And we shall resume it when and if the power is restored. Take a flashlight and go attend to it."

"I ain't no mechanic, I'm a guard."

"We are going to sit here in the dark unable to answer M. Tuluk's com unless somebody sees to the generator. Given that there are only two of us, it must be you or me, and for all we know it could be a burglar, so it's your job."

"Well, shit."

Cinch laid his carbine on the ground and rolled his shoulders a little to loosen them. There were people who would use the carbine to whack the guard on the head, but that was a terrible way to treat a fine weapon. Heads were hard, you could crack the stock or something.

A flashlight would blind him if he used the spookeyes. The flare shield would kick in and stay on as long as there were too many lumens hitting the lenses, but the ears would help him locate the guard.

Only two of them, that was good.

He heard the man coming, tromping his way along, and the beam of the light splashed over the interior of the shack, some of it filtering through the blue Everlast. He shut the wolf ears off when the guard got to within a couple of meters.

"Shit, Doc," the man yelled. "Looks like some kinda short, it's all burned up, stinks like hell. I'm thinking major repair here—"

The guard shut up suddenly as Cinch slipped up behind him and snapped his right arm around the startled man's neck, applying a pressure hold with his biceps and forearm to the carotid arteries.

The flow of blood to the guard's brain was effectively shut off.

The man struggled for five seconds, tried to yell and managed a croak, then started to go limp. Cinch held on until he was sure the man was out cold, then let him fall.

"What was that last you said?" came the yell from inside the shack. "After the major repair part?"

Cinch grinned, plucked the guard's weapons away and tossed them into the blueweed, then used the cuff tape he'd brought to bind the man's hands and ankles. He wouldn't be going anywhere immediately when he woke up.

Cinch nodded at his work, then collected his carbine and went to meet the man inside.

Hello-o-o, Doc. What's up?

"No response," Lobang said.

"Damn. Damn! Threaten the engine, would you?"

"I got the throttle squeezed tight now, boss. Top speed."

"Shit! It's the ranger. He's at the Twist shack."

"I dunno, boss, maybe it's just a coincidence or something."

"Maybe if you had a curly tail and a snout you'd be a mud-rooting babi. It's him, I know it. Get whoever you can get out there, *now.*"

Lobang opened his com and started talking, but Tuluk didn't have a lot of hope. Most of his men were wandering around at the burst pipeline, just as the damned ranger had wanted. Maybe if they hurried they could catch him, but if they didn't, they were going to have to find him, fast, before he could carry tales. And they were going to have to kill him. Even if that meant other rangers would come. He could dismantle the operation if he must; it would be a setback but it was better than the alternative.

God damn the fucking Stellar Rangers!

* * *

"Wh-Who are you?"

"Evening. I'm Cinch Carston, Stellar Rangers. And you?"

"Uh—uh, I—I'm, I'm Dr. Picobe. I—I'm in charge of blueweed operations."

"And not a very good liar, either," Cinch said. "Dr. Picobe, why would you need an armed guard here? Stealing blueweed wouldn't be all that easy, now, would it?"

"I—we, that is to say, we are working on an experimental strain of the weed; it—it is potentially very valuable."

"I see. And why might this strain of weed be so valuable?"

Picobe licked dry lips.

Cinch looked around. There was a bunch of chemistry stuff here, burners, tubes, some kind of reduction cooker, boxes of finely chopped and rendered weed.

"Dr. Picobe?"

"I—I am not at liberty to reveal my research. You understand."

Cinch grinned. "Oh, I understand. I think perhaps you ought to come along with me where we can discuss this at length, Doctor."

"Wh-Why? Why can't we talk here?"

"I think we might have company coming who might interrupt our conversation. Come along."

"I would rather not."

"I'm afraid I must insist." Cinch waved the carbine.

"This—This is kidnapping!"

"Not really. I'm exercising my authority as a ranger and arresting you."

"What for?"

"Well, I don't exactly know what the charge is yet, but I'm sure we'll find something. Move."

Picobe obeyed.

Cinch would have liked to have had a couple of hours to explore this place, to see if he could figure out what was going on. He moved to a rack of small vials and collected two of them, slipped them into his pocket as he marched Picobe out. The man would tell him what was going on, he was fairly certain he could persuade him of that. But they had to move out; he didn't think Tuluk was stupid, and it wouldn't take him long to realize the raj's attack had been a trick. By the time he got his men here, Cinch wanted to be well away with his prize. A live one who would tell him everything he wanted to know.

chapter 20

Tuluk's limo fanned down into the clearing and he and Lobang jumped out of the vehicle before it settled fully onto the ground.

The area was lit by several portable HT lamps on spindly stands, a garish glow whose effect was lessened somewhat by swarms of flying insects hurling themselves against the lights. Four members of his security team had already arrived. A man carrying a plasma rifle ran over to them.

"What's the situation here?" Lobang demanded.

"We found Bretél taped up out by the power shack. The generator housing is partially melted, generator's safetied out. Nobody else around, nothing missing, far as we can tell."

Lobang led Tuluk to where the guard Bretél stood, rubbing his wrists. "What the hell happened?" Lobang asked.

Bretél shook his head. "I dunno. Me 'n Picobe, we was in the shed and the power went out. I came out to check it, that's all I remember. I woke up taped in the dark and the team found me when I started yelling."

"Where is Picobe?" Tuluk said.

The man shook his head. "I dunno."

"Who did it?"

"I didn't see 'im. I don't even know what happened. My neck is sore."

Tuluk turned to Lobang. The bigger man said, "Choke hold. He stopped the blood from getting to his brain—not that much gets there on a good day, I bet."

"He has Picobe," Tuluk said.

"Yeah. Looks like."

Tuluk sighed. "Come on. We need to get the limo into the air."

"Huh?"

"Just do it."

Lobang followed him to the limo, talking. "Maybe we can track him. He couldn't have walked in so fast, you know. He's got to have a flier of some kind—hopper, flitter, softwing, something."

"Nobody saw it come in," Tuluk said. "Why would we see it leaving?"

They reached the limo. Tuluk slid into the back and opened the lockbox built into the seat in front of him. Lobang started the engine and took the limo up.

"Get to a thousand meters," Tuluk said, as he found the transmitter he wanted. He tapped a code into the device using the tiny keyboard, checked the numbers and letters on the thing's little screen to be certain it was the right one.

"How come?" Lobang said. "I mean, what good is going up to a thousand meters gonna do us? We'll never see him if he's hugging the ground."

"Just fly the car, Lobang, and let me do the thinking."

Lobang glanced into the rearview mirror, shrugged.

Tuluk stared into space. Once, when he'd been a young man of forty or so, he had gotten into a deal with a piratical dealer in pornographic sculpture. The man, Jenson Blanco Stone, had a double-dip racket going. First he would sell you a piece of erotica, usually obtained illegally or immorally or both, then he would blackmail you. Pay additional money or the word will get out that you collect such things. Naturally, he seldom stung the same client twice, but he was reputed to have made millions. This was revealed after his sudden and unexpected death from a fall off a balcony belonging to a mistress in Nanoc City's famed Red Thighs District. Fortunately for his clients, the bulk of his blackmail material vanished somehow. Unfortunately for Stone, he had chosen to try his game on Manis Tuluk, who didn't give a mouse turd if anybody knew he collected exotic erotica but who would not be held up by somebody he trusted, however slightly.

Tuluk had seldom enjoyed an expression on someone's face as he had that on Stone's as he shoved the blackmailer off the balcony.

Since then, Tuluk had taken pains to make sure those people who weren't within his personal grasp and who might be able to cause him irreparable damage were unlikely to do so.

"How high are we?" he asked Lobang.

"About seven hundred meters—uh oh."

"What?"

"I'm getting a yellow on my board here. Looks like something wrong with the left repellor equalizer. Maybe we better put back down and check it out, boss."

"Never mind. We're probably high enough. We don't want to wait until he's out of range."

Before Lobang could ask what *that* meant, Tuluk pushed the transmit button on the device he held, tapped it quickly four times.

"Boss?"

"Go ahead and land. I'm done here."

Cinch and his reluctant passenger sped through the dwindling night, ten meters high and at two hundred and fifty klicks an hour. The little flitter carried the two of them as easily as it had Cinch alone, and they were already fifty kilometers away from the blueweed shed where they'd met only fifteen minutes before.

"You okay back there?" Cinch yelled. He glanced at Picobe to be sure. The man was snugged into place with thigh straps and he clutched tightly at the passenger handle grips that jutted up in front of him.

Picobe said, "I don't care for this! I want a legal!"

Cinch grinned. But before he could look back at the air ahead of him, Picobe screamed. He groaned, his face contorted in a way Cinch would not have thought possible, mouth twisted, tongue stuck out, eyes wide and bulging.

"Picobe?"

The man's face went blank, just like that, and he slumped forward.

"Oh, shit!" Cinch said.

At the rendezvous point, Cinch watched as the raj, triumphant in their night's work, pulled the van to a halt. Pan jumped out, grinning, and came to where Cinch stood next to the flitter and the prone form of Picobe on the ground.

"Who's your friend?"

"That was Picobe, one of Tuluk's scientists."

"Was?"

"He's dead."

"Oh, man. What happened?"

"I don't know. Looks like he had a major stroke."

The other members of the raj drifted over and looked at the corpse.

"I don't think it was a natural death," Cinch said. "That would be real coincidental, happening when it did."

"So, what was it?"

"I don't know for sure. You have a medic you can trust?"

"Yeah. Lu'prezo, from Dry Springs, he doesn't have any love for Tuluk."

"Let's pay him a visit."

They loaded the van, putting Picobe's body in first. The raj avoided sitting close to it.

Cinch couldn't blame them. For them, this had all been a game so far, nobody had gotten killed. Picobe had been murdered, though, Cinch was pretty sure of that. He didn't know how, just yet, but he was going to find out.

"Now what?" Lobang asked. "The ranger's got Picobe, we're in trouble here."

"Picobe won't be telling any tales," Tuluk said. "But this place has got to be clean to the quantum level. Have everything broken down. Count the full-strength Twist vials and get them to Ulang. Tell him to stretch them because we are going to be a little behind schedule for the next delivery. Harvest the remaining Twist and burn it."

"Jesus, boss—"

"Do it. I've got the genetic encoders in my flash safe, nobody can open it but me without frying themselves and the contents. We are going to put this on hold until things cool down.

"Find the ranger, whatever it takes. Bring him to me, alive. We have to find out what he's said and to whom. After we know that, we'll get rid of him."

"Uh—"

"Listen, with the ranger dead and the operation cleaned out, nobody will be able to prove anything, even if they *know* what we had going, understand? A year from now, eighteen months, we start over."

Lobang nodded. "Okay. What about Picobe?"

"Picobe is dead, idiot."

Lobang blinked at him. "Dead? But—how?"

The medic was a gnarled old man, ninety-five if he was a day, and not bothered at all by the call from the raj in the early morning hours. "Hell," he said, "I don't sleep more than twenty minutes at a stretch anymore. Couple catnaps in the afternoon, couple at night, that's all I need. Lemme see the body."

Lu'prezo's office was in front of his house in Dry Springs. The town was an hour or so away from anywhere, the population maybe a hundred people, to judge by the number of houses, assuming there were a couple in each structure.

They put Picobe on the exam table and the medic went to work.

"We're not exactly state-of-the-art here," Lu'prezo said, "but we have a few toys."

He attached sensors to the body, wireless plugs and stikcaps, and went to his computer console. The unit was an old-style hand reader, and the medic waved his fingers at it expertly, giving it instructions. After a few moments, he nodded and turned to look at Cinch and Pan.

"Somebody blew his brain up," Lu'prezo said.

Pan blinked. "Huh? How?"

"You want to tell him or shall I?" the medic asked.

Cinch sighed. "Nano-implants. A biochem explosive injected into or sometimes ingested by a victim, made specific for nervous tissue. It accretes in the cerebellum and cerebrum. Somebody gave Picobe the stuff, a no-sting popper or maybe in his tea or something; he probably never knew he had it. Hit it with a certain frequency electromagnetic pulse and the explosive triggers. Enough to destroy a lot of very sensitive tissue."

"Christo!"

"Yeah. It is expensive, tricky to work with, hard to come by legally. I couldn't afford to buy it if I saved all my salary for three years. But it is perfect insurance for somebody who wants to make sure the recipient doesn't go telling tales."

"Tuluk," Pan said.

"Yeah. Picobe knew too much to be allowed to speak of it," Cinch said.

"He killed him, just like that."

"Yeah. It's getting really ugly."

"I can't believe it."

"Believe it. He's got something he doesn't want us to know about."

"What? What could be so valuable?"

Cinch pulled the two small vials he had collected at the blueweed shack. "We're going to find out. Doc, you have a chem scanner?"

"What do I look like, a witch doctor? Of course I have a scanner. It might not be good enough for the whites at a big medical center but it will sniff out just about anything anybody out here might be taking. What are you talking about here?"

Cinch waved the vials at the medic. "These."

He looked at Pan. "Let's see if we can find out what Tuluk has killed to keep hidden."

But before the medic could run the test, Cinch's com cheeped at him. Great, just what he needed.

"Yes?"

"Ranger, this is Gus Kohl. It's Baji. She's gone."

Cinch stared at the com.

Damn. It never rained but it fucking poured.

chapter 21

Given what he'd seen about Baji's behavior, Cinch wasn't all that alarmed; Pan, on the other hand, appeared to be disturbed greatly by her sudden disappearance.

"We've got to go find her!" he said.

Cinch looked at him. "It's a big planet. Where would you suggest we start looking? The two of us are supposed to crisscross the whole world and do that? Call her name?" He was a little irritated with Baji at the moment. It came out in his voice.

Pan ignored the sarcasm. "Town, for one. Maybe she was kidnapped by Tuluk!"

Cinch watched the old medic as he poured a sample from one of the vials into his analyzer. "Hold up a second. We know where Tuluk was a little while ago, he was out inspecting your little surprise. Besides, Gus Kohl said there weren't any signs of forced entry, plus one of his vehicles is gone."

"Where would she go in the middle of the night? Why would she just take off?"

The doctor's machinery hummed to life. The flat tubescreen it bore lit up with a crawl of numbers and a spike-bar graph.

"She was angry last time I saw her," Cinch said.

"Maybe she just went for a ride to blow off a little heat."

"Why was she upset?"

Cinch sighed. "She wasn't happy that your sister and I had become so . . . well acquainted."

"Why would that—?" he stopped and stared at Cinch.

"No," the ranger said, "I'm old enough to be her father. But maybe she might have thought otherwise."

Maybe, hell. But Pan here was smitten and it didn't cost anything for Cinch to make it sound questionable. No point in rubbing his nose in it.

Pan's jaw muscles danced as he clenched his teeth. Didn't help, Cinch's attempt at kindness. He thought the kid might want to take a swing at him and he wondered what his reason would be if he did: because he wouldn't sleep with Baji? Or because she wanted him to?

Pan held his temper; at least he didn't try to floor Cinch with a fist.

"I'm going to go look for her," Pan said. His voice was tight, stiff, and whatever affection he'd felt for Cinch was gone from his speech. He turned without another word and marched out.

Well, shit. What was he supposed to do? Baji was what she was, not his problem.

"My, my," the medic said. "Look at that."

"What is it?"

"You got yourself a major psychedelic here, Ranger. I could give you the chemical names, they run to half a page if I print 'em out, but you probably know it as 'Throb.' "

Cinch blinked. Now that was something he hadn't expected. An orgasmic mindchem.

"Judging from the trace elements, I'd say the stuff is being bioengineered and botanized."

"Which means?"

"It's been grown, Ranger. Created and cooked inside some variation of the local blueweed. A biological processing plant, at least for the first steps."

Cinch nodded. That explained a whole lot of things.

And didn't it make this whole affair real interesting all of a sudden.

Tuluk was angry at the turn of events, but in a strange, almost perverse way, he was happy. Okay, so he would have to put things on hold for a time. He would have to kill the ranger and weather the storm of investigation that would naturally follow. Those things would not have been his first choices by any means; still, it had been years since he had been forced to rise to any real challenge. A man missed that. Comfort was good, but it wasn't everything. Get too used to winning every hand, the game can get boring.

He sat in his study, sipping his imported whiskey. Been drinking more than normal lately, but certainly he was entitled. The problem with challenges was that they could be aggravating in their unpredictability.

Still, he was on top of it. Lobang and his collection of slow-wits had the illegal extract crated and on its way to a safe place, or damn well better in the next few hours. The Twist was being harvested and, regretfully, destroyed. It would make a nice series of fires and the resultant ash would be scattered. True, a good bioforensic tech could maybe come up with something to raise eyebrows—did she look in the right places even after the fires—but nothing to hang Tuluk with. Heat destroyed the active ingredients and "potentially illegal" didn't mean a thing.

Of course, this was only the beginning of the housecleaning. There was the ranger, that was a given. Gus Kohl would have to go, as would the damned raj, every last one of them. The woman Meritja, she might know something the ranger had let slip in his pillow talk. A broad broom, to be sure; but as long as he was sweeping, he might as well get it all. He would have to hire himself a new scientist. So many details. Ah, well. Life was in the details, was it not?

He sipped his drink and smiled.

* * *

Dawn came and went, the day blossomed into its usual heat and dryness. Cinch had left the medic's and gone off into a narrow canyon where he found a shady spot out of sight and parked the borrowed flitter. He located a soft patch—well, relatively soft, anyway—and stretched out for a nap.

He awoke a couple of hours later, made some coffee in the little hot pot, and felt a little more rested if not altogether fresh. Unless he was mistaken, Tuluk would now be a more dangerous opponent, and since he had demonstrated his willingness to kill, that meant Cinch would have to watch where he put his feet from now on. He didn't think there were going to be any more warning shots fired, and to expose himself without taking a few basic precautions would be stupid.

When he'd left Kohl's, Cinch had brought along a clean com unit. It was officially registered to a traveling sales rep for a food marketing chain halfway around the planet, the number and channel much different from Cinch's regular unit. The clean unit also had a scrambler and a bouncer on it. Anybody who might happen across it with a scanner would get an earful of white noise, and any attempt to backwalk it to a location should fail, unless the tracker had a program a lot better than most commercial ones available. He used the com now and called Wanita. Even if her channel was tapped, he could get away with a short conversation without being pinpointed by a listener.

He hoped.

"Yes?"

"Wanita, Cinch. You hear from Pan?"

She laughed. "Oh, yeah. When he came in, he didn't much like you, but he's a lot better now."

"Why is that?"

"I'll let him tell you. He's here. Hold on."

After a moment: "Cinch?"

"Yeah. You okay?"

"I'm fine. Better than fine. I'm great!"

"I take it you located Baji?"

"Oh, yeah, you might say that. I located her. She was waiting for me here when I got back. Look, Cinch, I'm sorry I was such a dickweed at the Doc's. I mean, I—well, Baji and I, we—that is, we've had a real nice visit and everything is okay. Great."

A real nice visit, eh? Cinch didn't have any trouble figuring out what that little euphemism meant.

Well, well. So Baji had found somebody else to play with. And from Pan's tone of voice, he'd thoroughly enjoyed being second choice. Gus Kohl might not like it, but Baji was in bed with the raj, at least in one way. Which was fine by him since it would keep her out of his hair. And maybe one less loose cannon would be rolling around the deck in such a way as to blow his head off.

"Glad to hear it," Cinch said.

"So what now?"

"I'm going to stay out of sight for a while. I'll put in a com to HQ and let them know what is going on here and then see what's what. You best cover your tracks. Tuluk and his boys will figure out who blew the pipeline and they'll be gunning for you. Be a good idea if you found a hole and stayed in it for a while."

Pan laughed and Cinch knew what he was thinking.

"That's not what I meant, Pan. This is serious. We might have scared Tuluk and scared men do stupid things. We'll stick him, eventually, but I would hate to see anybody get hurt until we do."

"I can take care of myself."

"Probably Picobe thought so, too. It's a discom, I'll talk to you later."

Ulang was not a happy man.

"I am sorry our agreement has to end this way," he said, his voice cool.

Tuluk shrugged. They met at a spot just outside of town. Lobang sat in the limo while the chem merchant and Tuluk stood in the shade of a cottonwood on the bank of a small stream. "It doesn't have to end, only be delayed for a time."

Ulang shook his head. "If the rangers suspect you, our further association holds no interest for me. You may escape prosecution by wiping away the ranger and those who could tell stories, but the rangers have very long memories. You might as well buy yourself a rearview cam and hang it on your shoulder, M. Tuluk. They might not be able to touch you legally, but somebody will be back there watching, you can bet on it."

"You are prone to hyperbole."

"No, I am a man wanted on a number of planets and I have seen how the rangers work, more than once. You are a rich man, most of it made legally if not morally. Enjoy what you have, Manis, because if you kill this ranger you'll never be able to step over the line again. They will come down on you like an asteroid on a moon without atmosphere. Trust me on this, M. Tuluk, I know. I have seen it happen too many times before."

Tuluk shrugged again. Ulang was skittish, he'd operated outside the light too long. Well. No matter. There were other dealers.

"I'm sorry you feel that way. No hard feelings?"

"Of course not. This is just business."

"I'm glad you understand," Tuluk said. "Oh, here, I have a little going away gift for you. You know the cigars you liked?"

With that, he drew his tangler. He took care not to move too quickly and thus alarm the dealer.

Before the Ulang's surprise had registered fully, Tuluk fired the weapon.

He could hardly have missed from two meters away. Ulang fell, his consciousness fled forever, his brain dead and his body hurrying to catch up.

Lobang scrambled from the limo and sprinted toward him, his own gun drawn.

"Christo, boss, what the hell happened?"

"He became tiresome."

Tuluk felt a small flash of triumph as he saw the astonishment in Lobang's eyes. Didn't know the old drone's stinger was so sharp, did you? See that you don't forget it.

"Get rid of the body," Tuluk said. "And be careful you don't blow yourself up with that explosive he supposedly has wrapped around himself."

The air smelled like roasted walnuts.

chapter 22

Tuluk thought about the problem with the same kind of focus that had made him rich. The solution was simple, in theory: Figure out what's broke and fix it.

He sat in his study, drinking coffee this time—he needed to keep his wits sharp now, this ranger had proven more adept than expected—and considered various plans.

He couldn't control all offworld communications, but he could exercise his considerable clout in monitoring message tubes headed for the Stellar Rangers' Sector HQ. So far, none had officially been logged since Picobe's abduction, and it was worth five years' pay to the man or woman who intercepted and delivered any such tubes to him. Certainly there were ways around this and Tuluk had to assume that eventually some word of what the ranger thought would get past. Could be hidden in freight or some such. But that was later. What he needed most now was enough time to clean house, and a few more days would ensure that. Even if the rangers had a ship standing offworld that could get here in a week or less—which he doubted—it would do them no good if there was nothing for them to find.

The ranger had to be found, made to talk, and then eliminated.

Anybody who might possibly know what he knew, or even suspected, would also have to be silenced.

Tuluk waved his com to life. "Lobang, I want you to bring in the mercenary group from Kingsland."

"Aw, boss, we don't need—"

Tuluk shook his head at the com. Maybe Lobang had outlived his usefulness. The stupid thug was really beginning to irritate him. "Just do it. I have a list of people I'll want rounded up."

"Okay, boss."

Tuluk waved the com off. All right. That started things. There was a fire, he would put it out and once things cooled, rebuild. A glitch, that was all.

In the shade of the overhang, Cinch finished dictating his report. Tuluk was hurrying, no doubt to cover his ass, and that wasn't good. Cinch's only real option was to put a stop to Tuluk's cleanup operation before it vanished completely. How he was going to do that exactly wasn't clear. He was outgunned and he wouldn't be able to get help from offworld for weeks, by which time it might be too late.

The report finished, he sealed it into its tube and stashed it in the flitter's carrier. So he had to figure out a way to stop Tuluk from wiping away whatever evidence there was, if he wanted to give galactic or local authorities something with which to build a case against the rich man. By himself. Odds on that didn't look real good, but he would work on ideas.

What else?

After a moment with the hot breeze from the desert washing over him, Cinch realized he'd forgotten something.

He put in a com to Wanita.

"What's up, Ranger?"

"It occurred to me that Tuluk is getting real nervous about now," he said, "and we know he's not above killing people. It would probably be a good idea for you to take a little vacation."

"Why? All I do is serve the man drinks."

"Until you started spending your spare time with me. He might play it conservative, just shut things down and wait until we get bored looking for evidence—that's what I would do in his place. But he knows I know what he's up to, and he might guess that you and Pan and Baji know, too. I expect him to try to take me out. That's part of the job and I know how to deal with it. But it worries me he might want to extend that to anybody I've talked to since I've been here.

"You and I, uh, we've done more than talk. We have to assume he knows that."

"I wouldn't put it past Lobang to peep in windows," she said. "But I've got a business to run and I'm not afraid of Tuluk."

"I didn't say you were afraid. Do it as a favor to me."

There was a long pause.

"Okay. I guess I can go see this hideout Pan is always bragging about. For a few days."

"Thanks. Take Baji with you. I'll talk to Kohl and let him know what's going on."

"You really think there's any danger?"

"I could say no, or I could coat it with a 'better safe than sorry,' but yeah, I think there is. Tuluk is rich and worried, and we know he is deadly. That makes him dangerous."

"Okay. You coming to see us there?"

"Maybe. But I don't want to know where it is until necessary."

"You *are* concerned about this."

"Just being careful. Make sure you aren't being followed when you go. I'll call you."

He discommed, then called Gus Kohl. The old man already knew his great-granddaughter was with Pan. He hadn't been happy to hear that but he didn't have a lot of choice in the matter. Cinch figured the girl was going to twist the old man's tail a lot more before she was done, unless he figured out a way to get a handle on her. Well. It wasn't his problem. Good thing, too.

Cinch explained the situation as he saw it.

"So, old Tuluk is finally going down."

"He won't go easy," Cinch said. "We know he's guilty but we still have to prove it. If I and everybody I talked to while I was here disappeared all of a sudden, it would make it real hard for anybody to prove anything. It would probably be a good idea for you to lay low for a while. Maybe go visit some distant relatives on the other side of the planet."

The old man made a rude sound. "Like hell I will. My boys and I will sharpen up our watch. I got shooters here who can knock a bucket off a stump at eight hundred meters."

"That may be true, but Tuluk already has spies on your property within spitting range of the house."

"You mean them two in the hidey holes with all the scopes and stuff? The ones s'posed to be watching you?"

"You knew they were there?"

"Son, this is my ranch. A cow farts and I know about it. Them two won't cause anybody any trouble, they'll be wrapped up tight in about three minutes from when I say so."

"Better say so, then."

"If Tuluk comes calling, we'll give him something to think about."

"It's your neck."

"That it is, son. You sure Baji is gonna be okay?"

"I trust Pan and Wanita. She'll be as safe with them as anywhere else. Can't hurt what you can't find."

"I guess so. All right. You keep me posted."

"I'll do that."

Cinch broke the convoluted radio connection. What else had he missed? Anything? He didn't think so, but he had a nagging worry he'd overlooked something, something obvious. He usually felt that way at some point in an operation and usually he was wrong, but it didn't make the next time any easier. In this game, one wrong move could cost you your neck.

The com cheeped at him.

"Cinch? It's Pan."

"What's up?"

"I have somebody here you need to talk to. Name is Sutera Kutjing."

"Yeah?"

"He says he's the partner of an illegal chem merchant who was here to cut a deal with Tuluk. Says his partner went to a final meeting and that Tuluk killed him."

"He's probably right."

"No probably about it, he says. His partner was a very cautious man and he set it up that if anything happened to him, he was to find you and deliver a package."

Cinch felt a rush of hope flow through him.

"A package?"

"Yep. According to Kutjang, it is a record of everything his partner and Tuluk set up, full audio and video of the whole deal."

Cinch grinned. Hard evidence? That Tuluk didn't know about? Proof of a conspiracy to manufacture and sell illegal drugs? Oh, that would be nice. Tuluk could run around vacuuming things until they sparkled like diamonds, could wipe away physical evidence until there was nothing left no way to get him on possession or manufacturing—but conspiracy, that was something else.

"Cinch?"

"Yeah, go ahead."

"Kutjang says the dead man took a remote with him at the last meeting with Tuluk and had it set up to transmit to a recorder. He says that's how he knows his partner is dead.

"He's got a recording of Tuluk murdering him."

chapter 23

Cinch arranged to meet up with the doper on the way to Pan's hideout.

They connected twenty klicks out of town to the southeast, in a dry wash bounded by tumbleweed and creosote bushes. Pan and Wanita were there, along with Baji and three other members of the raj. The van had been strung with camouflage electronics and should be hard to spot from the air.

They were playing it cautious, just as he'd advised them. Pan would probably be a lot more reckless if Baji hadn't been with them. The two of them stood next to each other, Pan with one brown arm draped casually around Baji, and she smiled at Cinch with a nasty look that dared him to say anything.

See? I can fuck Pan stupid. Too bad you didn't take it when it was offered.

Cinch repressed a shudder. If you're captured by the hostiles, don't let them give you to the women. . . .

Sutera Kutjing was a thin blonde, his hair worn long. His skin was pale under the shade of the wide-brimmed hat he wore, and his features were delicate, almost feminine. He wore blue osmotic skintights and looked more like a young boy than a man.

"I'm Carston," Cinch said.

"I wish I could say it was a pleasure to meet you, but

163

it isn't," Kutjing said. His voice was surprisingly deep but filled with sorrow. "I wish the opportunity had never happened."

"You and this man, Ulang, were . . . partners?"

"We were not *business* associates. Our connection was personal."

"I see. I'm sorry."

"He was a wanted man, a criminal, but he loved me and I loved him. We always knew it might end like this."

Cinch couldn't say he felt a lot of sorrow for the chem peddler's death, but Kutjing obviously did.

"I want you to punish the man who killed him. I have the means."

Cinch took the packet from the thin man and looked at it. It was a plastic case about the size of a man's hand.

"There are hardcast infoballs inside, all of the meetings with Tuluk including the last one. The bastard fried Zar's brain with a tangler and had his trained ape do something with the body, I don't know what, buried it, fed it to the lizards, shoved it into a grinder. It doesn't matter. I want the man who killed him to die for it."

Cinch looked at the plastic container. "I can't guarantee the death penalty but we'll come down on him as hard as we can. I take it you are willing to testify as to the authenticity of the recordings? You have seen them?"

"I watched them as they *happened*, Ranger. I *saw* him die. I'll testify."

Gotcha, Tuluk, Cinch thought.

"All right. I'd like you to stay with Pan until I can get some Galactic Marshals onplanet. It might take a couple of weeks but we have time now. The clock is on our side."

Pan said, "Aren't you worried about Tuluk running? He could be light-years away in two weeks."

Cinch shook his head. "He won't run, not yet. Really rich people never do unless things get really bad. They think they can bury anything if they shovel enough money over it. He doesn't know about this—" Cinch waved the case "—so while he's nervous, he probably thinks he has things under control. We can afford to sit tight and wait until the troops get here. A shipload of marshals in combat gear will make short work of his hired guns.

"Tuluk doesn't know it, but it's all over but the mop-up."

Tuluk reacted to the news with a cold dread. His belly twisted, and had the dealer Ulang been there he would have killed him again, only slower and with a lot more pain.

Damnation! How could he have missed being recorded?

Well. Truth was, he had never considered it. Why would somebody record something that would incriminate them equally? That was not very bright. As life insurance, it had failed; as revenge, the success had yet to be determined. But it did make him nervous. If he didn't stop the ranger and his allies and get that evidence before it fell into the hands of the authorities, Tuluk was going to be in shit up to his hairline.

It was time to move and decisively so.

"Lobang, get in here!"

"What's up?"

"The fat is in the fire. We have things to do."

Cinch's flight path took him south and then west. He made a long loop so as to get to town from a different direction. He arrived at Lembukota late in the afternoon, brought the flitter to a stop in front of the constable's office and alighted.

He loosened his pistol in his holster and wiped his hands on his pants before he started toward the door. He hadn't seen anybody following him but he had to assume people were looking for him. This little bit of business needed to be done quickly.

The afternoon's heat was made worse by the underclothing of stackweave cloned spidersilk he wore under his shirt and pants. Called a stopsuit, the material was denser than Kevlar and only half as heavy. Even with the trauma panels stitched in over his heart and groin, it was not all that uncomfortable, save for the extra warmth he didn't need. It wasn't perfect, the stopsuit, but it would protect him from most common hand-weapon projectiles, from the base of his neck to his ankles, and being a tad overheated was worth the safety factor.

The constable was surprised to see him when Cinch stepped into the office. The fat man sat in a chair with his feet propped on his desk, looking at a pornoproj that shimmered from a small set on his desk. Something with several women and a single man. A common enough fantasy.

Maling jerked his feet off the desk and slapped at the holoproj. The orgy vanished. "What the hell are doing, sneaking in here like that?"

"Sorry," Cinch said. "I just wanted to keep you up to date on my investigation. Professional courtesy."

Maling stared at him, eyes slitting narrower. "Yeah?"

"It seems that I'll be leaving your planet soon," Cinch continued. "I can't find any evidence that points at a culprit in the malicious doings at Gus Kohl's ranch."

"It's the raj," Maling said. "I could've told you that all along."

"Maybe, but I can't prove it. So there's no point in wasting my time here, is there? I'll be shipping out soon."

"How soon? I mean, uh, in the next couple of days or something?"

"Probably a couple of weeks. I'm going to take a little time off, a vacation."

"Here? On Roget? Why would you want to do that? Nobody comes here for a vacation."

"I like wide spaces. Maybe I'll do a little camping, hunting, fishing, like that. Then I'll be on my way."

"Well. Sorry you couldn't find what you came for. Feel free to drop by and visit before you go."

Cinch smiled and nodded, then turned and walked out. Probably this wouldn't do any good, this little misdirection, but you never knew. Maling was doubtlessly chuckling to himself about how the fucking Stellar Rangers weren't so hot, even as he put in a com to Tuluk. While Cinch didn't really believe it would convince Tuluk he was giving up and going home, it might puzzle him enough to make him wonder what Cinch was really up to.

Any stress he could pile on the man without revealing

what he had and what he planned to do would help. People who were off-balance sometimes fell down.

Cinch could feel hidden watchers eyeing his every move as he climbed onto the flitter and cranked the repellors up. He left town in a hurry. Anybody who might try to follow him would have a hell of a time managing it, certainly not without being spotted. If they did try to tail him, the flitter was fast enough to lose them.

But he was alone as he cleared the five-klick marker heading north. He put the flitter down and used his electronic sniffer on the vehicle. Nobody had bugged it while it was parked in town. He remounted, lifted, and shot off into the dwindling afternoon.

"You have lost what little mind you had," Tuluk said to Maling. The constable had come to see him at the ranch, all full of himself. The ranger was giving up and going home, he said.

"But—but M. Tuluk, he stood right there in my office and told me."

"And if he'd told you he could fly by spraying rocket fuel out of his ass, would you have believed that, too?"

"He's up to something," Lobang said.

"Of course he is up to something. He's trying to throw us off balance. It isn't going to work."

To the big man he said, "Are you ready to roll on the other thing?"

Lobang glanced at Maling. "Uh, yeah, that thing, we're ready."

"Then let's do it. Constable, go back to town and finish your pornoproj. We'll call you if we need you."

Maling looked startled. As if he thought how he spent his time was some kind of big secret. Probably children playing on the street knew all about the constable and his hobby. Lord, he was surrounded by idiots.

Cinch put in a com to Pan and gave him his location. "I'll camp here tonight," he said, "and do a little more poking around in the morning. I've stirred the pot a little, maybe that will help."

Pan said, "Okay. Uh . . . Cinch? About Baji . . ."

"What about her?"

"Uh, well, I want to, that is, I'm glad you didn't, you know . . ."

Cinch smiled at the com and the unseen Pan all those kilometers away. "She's a beautiful girl, Pan, but no offense, your sister is a lot more woman and a lot more to my taste."

"I'll tell her you said that."

"She already knows. My best to you and Baji."

"Thanks, Cinch."

He broke the com, still grinning. Don't thank me for that, kid. She might be more curse than blessing and I'm glad it's your lot and not mine.

chapter 24

Cinch felt pretty good. He had what he needed to put Tuluk away. His new friends were safe. This case was about wrapped up. So far, he was still alive and in one piece and outside of a few bruises in great shape. Things couldn't be much better. Yeah, it had been a little more complicated than he had first thought, but it was not the beginning that mattered in this business, it was how you finished it.

In the morning, he would leave his desert hiding spot and take the flitter to Neglefil, a town some two hundred klicks to the southeast, where he would ship his notes to HQ and ask for them to crank up the marshals. Probably Tuluk had eyes watching for anything addressed to the Stellar Rangers, so he'd use one of the drop addresses and have the message trans-shipped from there. That was always a possibility on these backrocket planets, that your mail might get intercepted, so the rangers had long since figured out a way around that.

The actual evidence given to him by the dead drug seller's lover he would keep close to hand. Even if nobody fiddled with the mail, things got lost accidentally all the time. He wouldn't risk his case on some bored tube sorter who might drop the evidence behind a desk somewhere.

His hiding place was in the foothills to the north, once

again using a rocky overhang to shield him from the sky. His camo-tent draped over the side like a lean-to completed the cover. Supposedly the big lizards didn't spend much time in the hill country, but he had a UV fence line set up in a semicircle around the base of the overhang. If something broke the light beam, it would set off an alarm.

Cinch opened the case containing the recordings. There were three shiny black hardcast infoballs nestled in soft plastic sockets. He pried one of them out and slipped it into his reader, punched the device on.

The tiny holoproj danced in the night air.

The image showed two men sitting in the back of a limo. The camera must have been softwired to follow Ulang, for it zoomed in until both he and Tuluk were clearly identifiable, visible from the shoulders up. The viewpoint was outside the vehicle and the angle through the window next to the dealer. It was dark, but the image was augmented so that it had a faint greenish tinge to what was a black-and-white recording. Good equipment. The voices were clear, Ulang must have had a transmitter on him.

"—cold out there," Ulang said.

"How did you—?"

"It is a big part of my business to be careful, M. Tuluk, and how I go about it is something I prefer to keep secret. I am wanted on several planets and some of the rewards are quite substantial."

"I understand."

Cinch nodded to himself as he listened to the two men exchang a few chest-thumpings about how dangerous each could be, and then got to the business at hand. That Tuluk was guilty of conspiracy to produce and market illegal chem was established. Any forensic scan of his hardcast ball would show it to be first-generation and an unaltered once-only, assuming Ulang's boyfriend hadn't messed with it. Cinch was pretty sure he hadn't. A good simadam could run a vox-match and even a retinal scan on the images and positively identify the speakers, did a record of them exist. Tuluk's mouth talking in his positively ID'd voice would likely be enough to convince a jury of his guilt. Certainly there were ways to fake such recordings, but with the eye-witness testimony that went along with this they had a strong case.

Cinch unplugged the first infoball and was about to load the second when the tiny alarm receiver he had quikstiked behind his right ear chirped at him.

Company.

He shoved the infoball back into its plastic nest and slipped the case into his pocket. He put the tiny holoproj unit down and grabbed his carbine. He duckwalked to the far edge of the tent, dropped to his belly, and crawled as quietly and as quickly as he could along the base of the cliff.

The invisible fence perimeter he'd set up was fifty meters away from the camp. The reflectors had been perched on rocks or hung in scrub brush high enough so a small animal like a rat or the local equivalent of a rabbit or snake could move under it without tripping the alarm. He hadn't wanted to be kept up all night by prairie dogs going to take a leak. Anything as big as an ularsinga—or a human—would break the beam.

As Cinch hustled away along the rocky ground he considered the likely causes of the alarm. Could have been something as simple as one of the sensors being knocked out of alignment. He'd put them into position with quikstik, but cooling rocks could shift, and a night bird could have landed on a limb and jiggled something.

Maybe a rabbit had chosen just the right time to hop and had interrupted the beam.

Could be one of the big lizards.

Could be a human.

Could be the god Prishina come to share his campfire and pose him the Riddle That Let A Man Directly Into Paradise, too.

Best he find out which, and quickly.

When he was twenty meters away from the lean-to of the camo-tent, he stopped. He plugged in his wolf ears and slid his spookeyes down. The night came alive with wind and rustlings and cracklings, the darkness flared into a bright, pale green.

He heard the footsteps first, then saw the figure crouched and moving toward the tent. It wasn't a rabbit and it wasn't a wandering god, either.

Somebody had found him.

Who? How?

Worry about that later, Cinch. Deal with the situation first.

He scanned the night, looking for other intruders, but did not see or hear any. The one creeping toward the tent made enough noise now that Cinch removed his augmentation as he circled in a crouch of his own, moving to get behind the stalker. If he had to shoot, he didn't want to go blind and deaf, even for the instant the audio and visual cutouts would deliver.

Just in time.

The man got to within five meters of the tent. He carried a shotgun, a semiautomatic, and he raised it and started blasting.

The booms were loud in the night. Four, five, six, seven of them, a hard sweeping with a steel broom that shredded the tent, *spanged* off the flitter and chewed at the rock and whatever gear he'd left behind.

Cinch thanked his fortune that he'd brought the case of infoballs with him when he'd moved out.

And that he *had* moved out. If he'd been under the tent, he'd be dead now.

The man started forward to check the results of his shooting.

Cinch crept closer, until he was within seven or eight meters of the figure.

"Move and you die," he said.

The man froze.

"Drop the weapon."

The shotgun clattered on the hard ground. Cinch reached up and pulled the spookeyes down. The starlight was enough to show him clearly who had come to assassinate him.

Maling!

"How did you find me?"

"You think because I'm a local I'm completely stupid, but you rangers don't know everything!"

Cinch was surprised, sure enough. He'd looked for a tail, high and low, and he was sure the flitter was clean. And yet, here was the constable, having just put seven rounds of sleetshot into Cinch's campsite. How in the hell had this drag-ass managed that?

"Nope, we don't know everything, you're right about that. Then again, who is it under the gun here?"

With his augmented vision, Cinch saw the man clench and unclench his hands. He wore a sidearm—Cinch had seen it earlier—but it was a snub-nosed compressed gas slugthrower, more a badge of office than a field combat piece. Oh, you could shoot somebody with it and even kill them, but it was more for show than real work, a shiny chunk of stainless steel or mat-hardchrome that could be worn on a belt day in and day out without discomfort. In the hands of an expert, the pistol could be dangerous out to a hundred meters but somehow Cinch doubted that Maling spent a lot of time at the range practicing. Still, he was only seven meters away and even a pisspoor shooter might hit a man-sized target at that distance.

"Lose the pistol," Cinch said. "And then we'll have a little chat."

He very much wanted to know how Maling had located him. If this lame excuse for a peace officer could find him, what might that mean if somebody *good* came after him?

Maling must have thought Cinch could see no better than he could in the darkness. Without the spookeyes, Cinch was probably a dimly viewed shape against the horizon. The constable started his reach for the handgun slowly, but once he had his finger near it, he snatched at the weapon.

"Don't do it!" Cinch yelled. "Drop it!"

Maling wasn't listening. He jerked the pistol from its holster. The spookeyes showed the weapon as a greenish bit of mirror, leaving phosphor trails as it came up—

"Drop it!" He didn't want to have to kill the man—

The *clump!* of the gas blowout was loud in the night. Maling didn't use the sights, but point shot, thrusting his hand out like a punch.

The slug caught Cinch square in the chest, right over the heart.

Even with the trauma plate under the stopsuit, it hurt, like being thumped with a hammer. A good shot under the circumstances.

Cinch dodged to his left as Maling fired twice more, and both slugs found him, each a little higher than the one before. Damn, maybe the bastard did practice!

His head wasn't bulletproof and Cinch's emergency override squashed all thoughts but one: stop him!

Cinch fired the carbine. The spookeyes' flare protection shutter kicked on for a quarter second and the world went dark. When the green field relit, Maling was still falling.

Cinch moved to the man. The high velocity projectile had punched him in the center of mass and gone through the sternum, taking a big chunk of his spine with it when it blew through his back. He wasn't wearing a vest, and it probably wouldn't have stopped the round anyway.

Maling shuddered and went limp.

Cinch checked the carotids. No pulse. Massive shock to the system did that sometimes.

Well, *shit.*

However the man had located Cinch was a secret he took with him when he left. That was worrisome.

Things got no better when he went to check on the flitter and his gear. The sleetshot pellets had blown out the left repellor, as well as big chunks of the fibercast body on the vehicle, and it wasn't going anywhere under its own power without more repair than Cinch could manage here with the few tools the flitter carried. Somebody's uncle was going to be real unhappy.

His bedroll was also ruined, the small holoproj was dead, as were his com units, both of them, and most of his food and water were also beyond usefulness.

Amazing what a shotgun could do at close range.

Maling hadn't walked out here, so he must have transportation nearby. Cinch wasn't all that happy about using it, but it was a long hike to anywhere and if Maling could find him, somebody else might.

And Tuluk might be able to locate the raj.

A search of the body failed to turn up a com, though he did find a keycard.

Cinch left the dead man where he lay and went looking for his ride. He found it half a klick away, parked under some scrub. It was the official law enforcement vehicle, a boxy patrol hopper that would seat six, the rear compartment a meshed caged for prisoners, the whole thing painted a distinctive blue and green with a large number "1" stenciled on the roof. There was a com unit mounted in the hopper but Cinch didn't think it was a good idea to use it, it was probably monitored.

He considered his choices.

He had just sent the local lawman into the Great Beyond. His own flitter was gravely wounded and his communications were dead. He had a cold feeling that Wanita and the raj were endangered and he wanted to warn them, but the com unit in the constable's vehicle would probably pipe itself directly to Tuluk's ears.

He wasn't exactly sure where the raj were hiding, although he thought he had a general idea.

What was his best course of action?

While it was still dark, he could drive the constable's hopper to a place close to where he figured Wanita and Pan were hiding, then put in a fast call. Even if Tuluk's troops overheard and traced the com, he could get to the raj before they did. Then they would all move, to somewhere far away. That seemed like a plan.

As to Maling, well, he hadn't been much of a peace officer. He couldn't get any deader than he was. Maybe he would serve some purpose by feeding the night creatures.

Cinch slid into the hopper, pushed the keycard into the slot, and started the engine. He let the engine rumble for a while until it came up to lifting speed. He engaged the repellors and the vehicle rose slowly until it was twenty meters up. He hit the blowers and sped off into the remains of the night.

chapter 25

Cinch had a general idea of where the raj were hiding out. From some of what Pan had said and what he filled in on his own, he thought he knew the heading and about how far away it might be. When he was where he thought he might be no more than thirty or forty minutes from his best estimate, Cinch put in a com to Pan's secret number.

"Yeah?"

"Pan, Cinch. I think maybe we might have some problems. I'm on my way. How do I get there from here? Just give me headings and distances, no coordinates."

With that, Cinch told Pan what landmarks he could see from where he held the hopper in a high and tight figure eight.

Pan rattled off turns and kilometerage.

It would take him about twenty minutes to reach the hideout from where he was now. Not a bad guess, considering.

Cinch broke the holding pattern and flew toward the raj's hole in the wall.

If he hadn't known where it was, Cinch would have missed it. The area was wooded, more so than he had seen before, although the trees weren't particularly tall, maybe ten to fifteen meters. Some kind of evergreen with a pyramidlike canopy and short needles for leaves. It wasn't much of a forest compared to jungle worlds he'd been on, but for local vegetation it was the champion. There were four or five patches of it, the largest of which was maybe five hundred meters wide by a thousand long; it was hard to tell from the air at night exactly.

Cinch dropped the hopper to a bare spot near the third such copse. One of the raj who was good with electronics had rigged electronic camouflage so that a house-sized tent was supposed to be hidden in the middle of the small wood. Even as he walked toward the still unseen tent, Cinch still couldn't see or hear anything to give them away. It was very quiet, no light visible. They were doing a good job here, Cinch thought. The night air had a pleasant, piney scent to it.

He finally spotted the tent and moved toward it. Fortunately there wasn't much in the way of undergrowth among the trees so he didn't have to look for a path.

When he was fifty meters away, Cinch felt a coldness in his belly, like he'd suddenly swallowed a lump of metal left out in deep vacuum.

Something was wrong.

For a tent with at least six or eight people in it, there ought to be more incidental sounds.

He stopped and moved behind the partial cover of one of the trees. This feeling didn't make any logical sense, but he'd learned a long time ago to trust it when it happened to him. If he were wrong, he'd feel a little foolish, maybe. If he were right, however, and he ignored it, he might feel a little dead.

He laid the carbine on the ground and used his sensory augmentation gear once again. The night lit up in spookeyes ghost-green; the sounds of trees creaking in a gentle wind came through the wolf ears. He retrieved his carbine and began a circle around the tent. With the ears working, his own movements sounded like an elephant stomping across walnut shells. Every few meters he would stop, hold his breath so that didn't interfere with the sound, and listen.

When he was twenty meters out, on the opposite side from where he'd landed the hopper, he sat with his back against a tree and watched the tent, breathing slowly and evenly, listening carefully between each inhalation and exhalation.

After another fifteen minutes, his caution paid off.

"Where the fuck is he? He shoulda been here by now." The voice was a whisper, kept low enough so anybody with normal hearing would not have picked it up this far away.

"Shut the fuck up," a second voice whispered in answer.

Cinch didn't know either of the speakers. What he did know was that they were waiting for him.

Damn.

What had happened? If they'd been there when he called Pan, surely the boy would have figured out a way to let him know they were being held captive? Cinch went over the conversation again. There hadn't been any strain in Pan's voice, things had been okay then, the ranger was fairly sure. He wasn't that good an actor.

So, in the twenty minutes between his call and his arrival, somebody had gotten here, taken control, and set up an ambush.

What about the raj? Wanita and Baji? Were they still in there? Tied up, gagged, knocked out, or worse? He had to know before he did anything dangerous. If they were in there and alive, he had to get them out in the same condition.

If they were dead, the men who killed them were going to be sorry they were ever born.

How to get the bushwhackers out without damaging the captives, if they were still there?

Cinch looked at the tent. It was a standard big dome configuration, large enough to sleep twenty people, draped over flexible carbon fiber rods that formed a springy framework. Two doors—he was looking at one of them—and the material was camouflage cloth set to match the ground and trees. The power source for the cloth would be somewhere in the base, a high-voltage, high-capacity solar battery, probably, with a little step generator for augmenting it when it couldn't get enough recharging time.

The tent fabric would be fire-resistant, but if he could locate the battery. . . .

It took less time than he thought it would. The battery was next to the door. Good.

Moving with great care, Cinch attached a popper to the battery. Of course, the tent fabric was between them, but a device that would generate enough heat to melt steel would burn through the cloth real quick. When the battery got hot enough, it would rupture. It shouldn't explode—the cast plastic cases were designed to let go at a safety seam so that wouldn't happen—but by the time it broke open the contents ought to start smoking pretty good and the smoke should stink like a live skunk-roast.

Cinch set the popper for two minutes and crawled away. He made a circle around the tent again, so he was watching the other door. When the battery melted, they weren't going to go toward it. He stretched out prone and aimed his carbine at the door.

"—the fuck is that?"

"—Jesus, the tent is on fire, it's a short in the goddamn power!"

The tent's front door, a thick flap of cloth, snapped open. Four men ran out, and greasy black smoke boiled out through the opening with them. Two of the men were coughing, one cursing loudly, and the fourth came out crouched, waving a submachine plasma rifle back and forth in short, flat arcs, looking for a target. All four wore full military-grade body armor, helmets, visors, and bulky suits that covered them from chest to boots. The only target effective target area was from their mouths to the bases of their necks.

Cinch was twenty-five meters out and the protective gear they wore would stop anything he could throw at them, even his armor-piercing bullets, which he hadn't loaded.

Standard procedure called for him to identify himself as a ranger and order them to drop their weapons. Standard procedure here would get him killed. These were mercenaries, rigged for combat, and if he gave away his position, the alert one with the submachine gun would chop him into pieces.

His friends and lover could be in there. They might be dead. If they were alive, he had to get past this quad to rescue them. He had no choice.

All of this took maybe a second for Cinch to recognize and decide upon.

He put the sighting dot on the lips of the submachine gunner and fired. The flare shield in the spookeyes blinked and blanked the scene, but he had already begun to swing the carbine to the left a hair, and when the eyes lit again he lined the dot up on the second man's throat and fired again. Then he rolled, covering three meters until he slammed into a tree. He scooted behind the base of the trunk.

The other two troopers oriented themselves toward his muzzle flash and opened up with their weapons. The automatic fire lit the night and Cinch jerked the spookeyes off. The continuous flares would keep the shutters up to protect his eyes and he'd be blind. It didn't matter that the wolf ears had shut his sound input off, turning the roar of gunfire into the cracks of sticks breaking.

The muzzle blasts of the gunners were enough for him to see his targets. He aimed at the jaw of the third man and fired.

The fourth gunner swung his gun around. Bullets chewed at the tree as Cinch rolled to the opposite side, bark splashed like water; he felt the impacts of the metal pellets against the wood vibrate into his belly as he finished the roll and aimed at the last gunner. He fired, missed, fired again, missed—

A round from the armored trooper's gun smashed into Cinch's carbine. Like most men under fire, the hired gunner aimed at the perceived threat, in this case, the muzzle flashes of Cinch's weapon.

The shot wrenched the carbine from Cinch's grip, nearly breaking his trigger finger as it did so.

Cinch rolled again, moving back to the other side of the tree, snatching his pistol from its holster. He stretched his arms out, lined up on the patch of pale skin visible between the helmet's blast visor and the upper edge of the collarbone armor plate. Cinch fired, once, twice, three times—

The trooper fell backward, hit the tent flap, and went through it.

Smoke continued to pour from the tent.

Cinch came up from his prone position and ran in a half crouch to where the four men lay. It didn't take long to determine they were all dead. A high-velocity rifle round to the face or throat was usually fatal, hydrostatic shock and wound cavity being pretty severe. The last shooter had taken at least two of the three bullets from Cinch's pistol. One had gone under the shield, probably as he was falling, and hit him next to the left eye.

He held his breath and moved into the tent, keeping low. The smoke was thick and acrid, but he was able to see what he needed to see:

The tent was empty.

Outside again, Cinch reloaded his pistol and holstered it. He had four dead men and his friends and allies were gone.

What the hell had happened here?

What was going on?

This was wrong. How had Tuluk's men gotten here ahead of him? Quick enough to capture everybody, get them away, then set up a trap?

Too much coincidence. First, the constable had found him, now this. It didn't make sense, except for one reason Cinch didn't want to believe it. But he couldn't ignore it:

Somebody in their group was a traitor.

chapter 26

When the sun broke night's grip and there had been no call from the mercenaries declaring success, Tuluk assumed that the ranger had either bypassed the meeting at the tent in the woods or proved more adept than those lying in wait for him. Given his successes thus far, the latter seemed a distinct possibility.

He had Lobang put in a com to the merks. They weren't, it seemed, answering their calls just at the moment.

Score another point for the ranger, then.

Oh, well. It didn't matter. He still had the trump card in his hand.

Tuluk smiled as he activated the com. Getting the code from the leader of the dreaded raj had been simple, all it had taken was to point his tangler at the boy's sister and threaten to use it. These fools had over-reached themselves and now they knew who was in control.

"Yes," came the voice from the com. No surprise, no question in it.

Tuluk leaned back in his chair. Lobang and two of his men had the captives in another room, out of earshot, but it wouldn't have mattered if they overheard the conversation. When all was said and done, they wouldn't be telling anybody anything.

"Good morning, Ranger."

There was no preamble: "What do you want?"

"I would like to conduct a little business. You have something I want. I have something you want. Perhaps a trade might be in order?"

"Your four men for the raj and the others?"

Tuluk laughed. "Don't be absurd. If those four are alive, they are inept and worthless. If they aren't still among the living, you can feed them to the carrion birds. You know what I am speaking about."

"So the deal is, I give you the recordings and you let my people go, is that it?"

"It's a bargain. It's the only game in town."

"I'll think about it and call you back."

Tuluk frowned at the com as the carrier wave shut off. He had the upper hand here, how dare the man act this way? He was a ranger, he couldn't let the captives die. Now what was he up to?

He called to Lobang: "Bring Kohl's great-granddaughter in here."

There came the sound of a scuffle. After a moment, Lobang came into the room, leading Baji. Tuluk raised an eyebrow.

"The dreaded leader of the raj objected," Lobang said. "He's taking a little nap now."

"Leave us."

Lobang left the room, closing the door carefully behind him.

Tuluk looked at the girl. Quite beautiful.

"Take off your clothes," he said.

Cinch pushed the constable's hopper for all it was worth, heading for Gus Kohl's ranch. He was going to need help and that was the only place he was likely to find any he could trust.

He called ahead so Kohl's men wouldn't shoot him down.

When he arrived at the ranch, Kohl, wearing a holstered handgun and carrying an antique bolt-action hunting rifle—a thing of stainless steel with a wood stock—met him before he got two meters from the hopper.

"What's the problem?"

"Tuluk has Wanita and Pan and some of the raj, as well as the dope dealer's boyfriend. And he's got Baji, too."

"Damn!" The old man shook his head. "Well, I guess we'll just have to go and pry them out."

"That's not the best way, Gus."

"Son, if I let anything happen to Baji without doing something about it, I wouldn't ever be able to pass a mirror again."

Cinch took a deep breath. This wasn't going to be easy.

"Baji isn't in any danger," he said. "It's the others I'm worried about."

"I don't follow you."

Cinch sighed.

Tuluk had lowered the chair's arms along with his own pants and now the naked woman sat straddling his lap, moving up and down on him slowly.

She giggled and kissed the top of his head.

Tuluk smiled in return, looking up at those young and perfect breasts bobbing up and down.

"Can I have some of the stuff?" she asked, continuing her ride.

"In a little while. We don't want to get too active in here." He nodded at the closed door. "The game isn't quite over. We may need them to think you're one of them yet."

"They don't suspect a thing," Baji said. "Pan, poor Pan, he thinks I love him. After one session in bed, he would do anything I asked him."

"I can understand that. He's a hot-blooded young man." He leaned back and enjoyed the wet friction. Ah.

"He's just a kid. Not like you, Manny."

Tuluk smiled again. He didn't allow anybody to call him that, but given the current ... connection, he let it pass.

She leaned back and little and forced him deeper into her, raising her feet to prop them on the sides of his hips and holding onto the chair's back to give herself better leverage. She moaned a little.

Together they made little squishy, slurpy sounds. Getting a little faster now.

She wanted the chem. How much of her passion was faked at the moment he couldn't tell, but she would do anything for more of the drug that made the passion totally real. He had already decided that when this was all over with, he was going to keep her. She was too fresh and beautiful to let get away, especially when he had the hold on her he did. Kohl would be gone and Baji's father was offworld. Besides, she was of legal age, and she did stir him pretty good, even without the drug filling her.

He gave himself up to the pleasure beginning to build to a release in him.

"I don't believe it," Gus Kohl said.

They had moved into the shade of the porch, but neither Kohl nor Cinch sat.

"I'm sorry. But it makes sense."

"That somebody was passing information to Tuluk, yeah, I can see that. But not Baji. Pan or Wanita or one of the raj, maybe even the dealer's lover, you didn't check him out, he could be a plant!"

Cinch allowed the older man to vent his emotion. But he couldn't let it go without laying it out as best he could. He said, "I wish it wasn't so, but there are a lot of little things that add up, now that I think about them. First, I couldn't go to the fresher around here without Baji asking me when I was going and what I planned to do while I was in there."

"Hell, son, curiosity—"

"Let me finish. Second, it had to be somebody at the tent hideout who called in Tuluk's men. Nobody followed me from town but the constable found me, in the dark and under camouflage. He couldn't have done it alone and nobody knew where I was except Pan. And what Pan knew, Baji could have with a smile and a raised eyebrow. He would give his balls to her if she asked him for them."

"So, Pan—"

Cinch didn't let him finish. "I have reason to trust Pan and Wanita, they've shown me where they stand. They had the doper's boyfriend searched pretty carefully and he wasn't carrying a com or wired for casting. That leaves four or five members of the raj as possibilities, but none of them stood in front of me and told me how sorry I was going to be for crossing them. You were there when Baji did it."

"She was pissed off because you wouldn't sleep with her."

"Maybe. And maybe the reason she wanted me to sleep with her wasn't because I am so damned irresistible, but because she was told to do it. So she could find out what I was up to."

Kohl took a deep breath and blew it out. "It still don't scan, son. Baji wouldn't go against her own for Tuluk in this bidness."

"Maybe you're right, under normal circumstances. But Tuluk has a stockpile of one of the most potent psychedelic drugs known, a chem people are willing to give big money for, and if they don't have the money, have been willing to kill for. It isn't supposed to be physically addictive, but from what I've heard, nobody walks away from it once they've tried it. Tuluk could have used it on Baji. I'd be willing to bet he has."

"The son of a bitch! I'll kill him!"

"I'm inclined to let you do just that. But we have to get the hostages away from him before we can risk it."

Kohl sighed again. "Yeah. You got any ideas?"

"I think so."

"Let's get inside out of the heat and figure it out."

Cinch followed Kohl inside. He was glad he was not in the older man's shoes right at the moment.

And he wouldn't want to be in Tuluk's shoes if Gus Kohl got within rifle range of him, either.

chapter 27

"I dunno, son, it sounds real iffy."

Cinch nodded at the older man. They sat in front of the computer console in Kohl's office, staring at the map floating in the air.

"No argument here," Cinch said. "But I don't see any other choice."

Kohl rubbed at his face with one hand.

Cinch had a pretty good idea of what he was thinking. He said, "If I thought swapping the recordings for the hostages would work, I'd do it and let you shoot Tuluk later. But he can't let them go. Can't let them run around, knowing what they know. Or us, either, you and me. Here's how I see it. I call him and offer to make the trade, he'll ask for you and me to come alone to meet him somewhere, away from prying eyes. He'll say he wants to see the recordings first, then he'll let the hostages go. After he has the infoballs, you and I are past tense."

"You think Baji and the others are still alive?"

"Yes. He'll figure we won't want to hand over the information unless we are sure they are. So, just in case we get sneaky and hide the recordings, he'll keep the prisoners in one piece until he gets his hands on what he wants. He'll offer to let us com them to make sure they are okay, then he'll demand the infoballs. Once he is sure they are what they're supposed to be . . ." Cinch made a throat-cutting gesture with one finger.

"You're assuming an awful lot about a man you've only met one time."

"You have known him for most of your life, Gus. Do you think I'm wrong?"

The older man shook his head. "No, I think you're probably right." He stared into space at nothing. "All right. Call him."

Tuluk made himself wait until the com's alert chimed three times before he picked up the transceiver. "Yes?"

"All right," the ranger said. "You've got a deal."

Tuluk smiled. "Wise choice. Here's the scenario. You will meet me at Three Trees Junction in two hours. Come alone—no, wait, bring Gus Kohl with you, and bring the hardcasts and any copies you might have made."

"You'll bring the hostages?"

"Don't be stupid. We won't have any of those ranger heroics, blazing guns and that kind of crap. My . . . guests will be kept in a safe place until I am sure of your end of the deal. If all goes well, they'll be released."

"Why should I trust you?"

"Because I have the higher hand and you have no choice."

"Where is this Three Trees Junction?"

"About a hundred kilometers west of my ranch. Check your computer's map."

"Two hours, you said."

"That I did. Discom."

Tuluk smiled at the com as he cradled it in its recharger. He'd had a few bad moments after the first communication with the ranger, but he was back in control now. Already a dozen men would be nearing Three Trees Junction, which was nothing more than a joining of two surface roads in the middle of nowhere. He chose it because there was a thick stand of evergreens surrounding the clearing that bracketed the crossroads, offering plenty of cover for an ambush. With the hostages tied and guarded here, he and Lobang could collect the recordings and then have

Kohl and the ranger deleted at Three Trees and the bodies disposed of there. Several pods of ularsinga were known to roam the area, and they didn't mind if their meat was dead before they consumed it.

By the time the rangers got around to sending somebody to look for their missing member, anybody who could point a finger at Tuluk would no longer have the ability to do so.

While he was glad to be in control once again, there was a certain amount of unhappiness blended in. It should never have gotten to this point. Messy, full of the unpleasant business of having to dispose of all these bodies. It wasn't the killing that bothered him, but that it had come to the point it was required.

Ah, well. It would be over soon and he could start with a clean slate. Better that than the alternative.

"Lobang!"

"Yeah, boss?"

"Get the limo."

He could have stayed here, even Lobang had suggested that, but he had to be sure the ranger was out of the way and the information he tendered was what it purported to be. Besides, he wanted to see Gustav Kohl depart this world. He should have taken care of that years ago and it was his fault all this had come to pass as it had. He owed the old man that much, to take him out personally.

Tuluk checked his tangler, saw that it held three fresh charges, and stood.

As he walked past the room where the hostages were held he pulled the guard on the door aside. "I will call you when it is time. Keep them alive until I tell you."

"Yessir."

Confident that he had covered all his bets, Tuluk headed for the limo.

He wished his father were still alive to see him handling this crisis the way he was handling it. The old man had always thought his son was weak, that he would never amount to a dry white dog turd. He'd lived long enough to see the first million stack up in Tuluk's bank account and that should have been the end of the old man's carping, but it hadn't been. Even after he had proved himself, Tuluk's father wouldn't let it go. "Making a few coins ain't the same as keeping 'em, Manny. You ain't got the killer instinct. You fold up too fast when things get dilly."

He was a millionaire so many times over now he couldn't spend it all if he changed it into tenth coins and hauled a truckload away every day from now until he died of old age. Even the old man couldn't miss that, he wasn't rotting in a jar in a marble tomb. And Manis Tuluk had certainly shown the universe he wasn't going to fold when a stray breeze blew past.

No. It was risky, this walk on the high wire, but he was doing it and he was going to make it to the other side, just like he always made it before. It was just too bad the old man wasn't here to eat his words.

"Think they'll pass?" Kohl asked.

Cinch looked at the two men who stood before them. One wore some of the ranger's clothes and was the right size and coloring. The other was younger than Gus but was tan, had powdered or somehow whitened his hair, and wore the man's hat. From a distance, somebody looking for Cinch and Kohl would probably be fooled, since they wouldn't be leaving the GE car until it didn't matter.

"They'll do."

He said to the two men, "You make sure you arrive at the site exactly on time. You understand how it's supposed to go down?"

Both men nodded.

"All right. Good luck."

Cinch turned back to Gus. "All right. Let's get it moving."

Cinch led Gus out behind the garage. The hands had rigged the ranch's ancient turbine helicopter for the flight. Attached to the struts were two motorcycles. Gus was right, this was iffy, but he didn't see any way around it. He never considered asking Gus to stay behind. He was past his prime, but Cinch guessed he could still ride a bike or a horse all day and dance all night if it came to that.

"You want to fly it?" Kohl asked.

"It's your bird, you know it better than I do."

"All right."

The two men climbed into the craft. Cinch wore his stopsuit under his clothes, and Kohl wore his spare vest—he couldn't get into the shirt or pants or Cinch would have have had him use them. Kohl carried his hunting rifle and Cinch his own antique handgun. If he had to do any shooting it would be at close range, he figured, and speed would be important. He was faster with a pistol than a rifle. What he wished was he wouldn't have to shoot at all, but he didn't expect that.

This was all going to come down to timing. *If* everybody did exactly what they were supposed to do precisely *when* they were supposed to do it, he figured he had maybe a 50 percent chance of saving some or all of the hostages. Not real good odds when your life was on the line, but better than the certain alternative.

The rotor began to spin, the long blade whirling overhead. It was loud, despite the noise dampers in the cab. Dust blew up around them as the copter lifted. Kohl pivoted the bird and angled off toward the west, keeping the craft only a few meters off the ground. Cinch took deep breaths to steady himself, but his pulse was racing to rival the flying copter.

Death had drawn a line in the dirt with the toe of His boot once again, and it was time to step across the line and see what happened.

"How far?" Tuluk asked.

"About fifteen klicks. Be there in about five minutes."

"Our men are in place?"

"Yeah, been there for almost an hour now."

"Good. They understand that nobody does anything until I give the signal?"

"They understand. You take off your hat and wipe your forehead with the back of your hand."

"Any sign of Kohl and the ranger?"

"No. We got a watcher hidden on the Lower Lizard Road, that'll be the way they'll come, about twenty klicks out from Three Trees. He'll call when he sees them."

Tuluk nodded and stared at the ground passing by. He felt excitement gripping him, turning his bowels fluttery and sending chilly ripples through him. This wasn't all bad, there was a silver lining to this cloud. It had been awhile since he had felt this way, and he leaned into the feeling. He enjoyed this anticipation, the hunt leading to the kill. He needed to do it more often, he realized. Starting the Twist project had begun making him feel the power again. Killing the drug merchant had further sparked it in him. Having sex with Baji Kohl brought him to it in another way. Things like that helped to keep a man's wits sharp, his taste for life fresher. He had been sitting around too much before all this happened, he realized, and getting stale. Resting too comfortably on his wealth.

Well. No more. He wasn't that old. It was too early to sit back and watch the cattle graze. He would find other ways to keep the new fire blazing. Whatever it took.

Cinch looked at the copter's chronometer, then at his own, seeing that they were in synch. Kohl had the little craft zipping along at maybe three meters up, fanning big clouds of dust behind them. The way the wind blew out here, it was likely nobody would notice it, especially this far away.

"How close?"

"Getting near the horizon line," Kohl said.

"Okay. Stay at least a klick back."

Kohl had told Cinch that Tuluk's house radar was a standard set sold to civilians for nonmilitary uses. In theory, the ground clutter below the horizon should fuzz their image enough so somebody on a scope wouldn't be able to resolve it in time. After that, well, they'd have something else to watch and they'd have to be blind to miss.

"Going to put her down right there," Kohl said, pointing.

Cinch nodded.

Kohl landed the copter. Both men hopped out and began to untie the motorcycles strapped to the landing struts. It only took a minute or so.

When the bikes were free and moved, Kohl reached

back into the copter for his rifle and a flatscreen remote control that had been plugged into the copter's board. He moved over to stand next to Cinch.

"Now we wait," Cinch said.

At the meeting site, the outside heat fought against the open window in the back of the limo, but lost. The cooler kept the hot air mostly at bay.

"Call coming in from our watcher," Lobang said. "They just passed over him."

"He sure it's them?"

"Kohl's GE car, two men only, one with white hair, the other wearing the ranger's light-colored hat."

"Good. Tell our men in the woods to get ready."

"They're ready."

"Tell them anyway."

"Okay, go," Cinch said.

Kohl touched a control on the flatscreen and the copter took off and spun away, rising rapidly.

"I see the ranch house," Kohl said. He played with other controls. "I got the arc locked in. Two minutes."

"Let's roll."

The two of them hopped onto the bikes and roared off.

"Call coming in from the ranch, boss."

"Put it on the speaker."

"M. Tuluk?" It was one of the guards he'd left behind. "What?"

"We got a UAC on the radar. Looks like a hopper or copter."

"Where?"

"It's climbing through five thousand meters on the eastern edge of the property."

"Heading toward the ranch house?"

"No, it's veering away."

Tuluk chewed at his lip. Was the ranger up to something? He had to know the hostages would die if he did anything stupid—

"Heads up, boss. GE car coming in."

Tuluk glanced through the window. Yes, that was Kohl's car and there they were inside, just the two of them. Too far away to see their faces for sure, but it looked like them.

To the guard he said, "All right, keep an eye on the flier. If it heads toward the house, call me."

Cinch set the pace, hoping Kohl was staying with him. He didn't dare look back. The ground was tricky and he could not afford to hit something and be thrown from the cycle, not only because it would probably break his neck, but also because it would fuck up the timing too much to recover.

The bike bounded over the dirt, the little engine quiet but working hard. The goggles kept the dust from his eyes, but the clear plastic was getting grimy. He risked a quick swipe to clear them.

Ahead, the house loomed. Only a couple of klicks now.

Cinch glanced up, looking for the copter. There, there it was, to his left. No longer climbing, it was coming down again.

It was coming down fast. Very fast.

Tuluk watched the GE car fanned to a stop. When the dust settled, the car was a hundred meters away from the limo. Neither of the men inside made any move to exit.

"What are they waiting for?"

"Dunno, boss. Maybe they're cautious. They got reason to be."

"All right. Move the limo closer."

The com chimed again. Lobang answered it. "Yeah?"

"Anjing? This is Putin. We got a situation here. That aircraft is heading for the ground about a klick out and it's coming down like a fucking rock—holy shit!"

"Putin? What?"

Tuluk heard the explosion through the com and it was loud. It must have rattled the plastic windows half out of their frames at the ranch. Simultaneously with the noise, the guard started spewing words. "Christo, the ship crashed! It went off like a fucking bomb, Zeezus, there's a cloud of smoke and fire like you wouldn't believe!"

Tuluk heard a babble of other voices behind the one called Putin:

"—nobody's walking away from *that!*"

"—fuck, look at that cocksucker burn!"

"—man, oh, man, lookit!"

Before Tuluk could think of what to tell the guards, Lobang said, "Uh oh."

The ranger and Kohl had gotten out of their car and both had weapons. They were pointing them into the woods.

"What do they think they're doing?" Tuluk said.

Cinch thumbed his com and said, "Okay, boys, make some noise. Good luck."

"Gotcha," the man pretending to be Cinch replied. "Good luck yourself!"

Cinch risked a look behind him. Kohl was no more than five meters back on his cycle, covered with dust, hunched low over the handlebars. Good. They were only a hundred meters from the house. The smoke from the explosives in the helicopter boiled high into the sky, easily visible even on the opposite side of the ranch house.

When he was thirty meters away, Cinch stood on the brakes. The bike slewed to the left and skidded to a stop, throwing a cloudy sheet of red-brown dirt as it stopped. Cinch dropped the bike and ran toward the rear door. He had a shaped charge ready in his hand. Slap it on the lock and it would shear the bolt like a knife through cobwebs. The noise wouldn't matter, it was speed that counted now.

Just to be sure, Cinch grabbed the door's handle and twisted.

The door opened. Damn. Not even locked. He grinned and tossed the charge aside, thanking Fate for small favors.

Gus Kohl was right behind him as he darted into the house.

The ranger and Kohl started shooting into the woods. "Shit!" Tuluk yelled. "This is crazy!"

Lobang fumbled in the dashbox and came out with a small monocular. He looked at the two men shooting. "It ain't them," he said.

"What?"

"Not Kohl and the ranger."

"Give me that!"

Lobang handed Tuluk the monocular. He held it up to his left eye, waited for a second while it refocused. There were the two men blasting at the woods. Whoever they were, they were *not* the ranger and Kohl.

"Fuck!"

"Boss?"

"Tell our men to return fire! Shoot them!"

Lobang reached for the com control.

Three hoppers roared into view. Tuluk stared at the new arrivals. Where the hell had they come from? What was going on here?

Men leaned from the open hopper windows and fired rifles or pistols into the woods. One of the hoppers flew toward the limo, also shooting. Something *spanged* against the limo's armor, another round splashed against the AT glass windshield, leaving a gray-and-orange spatter that looked like a giant bug had hit the bulletproof material at speed.

"Goddammit! Get us out of there!"

Lobang started the engine and jerked the limo into a fast lift and turn. Tuluk was thrown back against the seat. Only then did he remember the hostages.

"Call the ranch! Tell the guards to kill the prisoners!"

"I'm kind of busy here!" The limo swerved to avoid being smashed by the incoming hopper, a vehicle full of men firing guns and obviously trying to either blast them, hit them with their vehicle, or both.

"Aahh!" Tuluk couldn't stop the scream as the hopper shot past, missing by centimeters. More gray flowers blossomed against the limo's windows. Tuluk hurried to power up the open window next to him, on the opposite side from the hopper.

The ranger was crazy! What did he hope to gain with this stunt?

* * *

Cinch went in low, his pistol held tightly in his right hand, a spare magazine for it clutched in his left. He ran through the kitchen and down a hallway.

A man stepped out at the other end of the hall. He had a shotgun. Before he could bring it up Cinch shot him, pointing his pistol like his finger and poking at the man's chest. The man threw the shotgun into the air and collapsed.

"Go to the left!" Kohl yelled.

Cinch cut through the doorway Kohl indicated. Kohl knew the house; they had discussed where the hostages were likely to be kept. It was guesswork, but all they could do. Since there were seven or eight of them at the least, plus maybe guards, Tuluk would probably have them in a big room.

To his left, down a second hall, another man materialized. Cinch shot him, twice. He didn't bother to look at the man's face. The hostages wouldn't be running around loose, anybody else was dangerous.

While he was running, Cinch dropped the magazine from his pistol and shoved the second mag in, a tactical reload. Now he had seven rounds. He had another magazine in his belt, but he hoped he wouldn't need it.

The rifle boomed behind him. Cinch glanced back and saw a man falling from a doorway, smoke still hanging in the air from Gus's shot.

Ahead, a fourth man came out of a room, a carbine held at waist level. Cinch brought his pistol around, but too slow. The man fired a round before Cinch got lined up.

The round missed, but behind him, Gus grunted and swore.

Before Cinch could shoot, Pan sailed out of the doorway and into the man with the carbine. Pan's hands were tied behind him but he smashed into the guard with his shoulder and body, knocking them both sprawling.

Cinch slid to a stop, pointed his pistol at the downed man. "Don't fucking move!"

The man's head had gone through the thin wallboard six

centimeters off the floor. He wasn't going to be moving any time real soon.

The ranger flicked a glance into the room and jerked his head back just as fast. No sign of a guard inside, but Baji and the others were there, alive and tied. He turned to look at Kohl. "They're here, they're okay!"

The older man had his left hand clamped onto his upper right arm. "Thank God." He shook his head, looked at his arm. "Bullet went right through," he said. "I think it clipped the bone a little, but I'm okay."

From the floor, Pan said, "One of them's got Wanita! I don't know where he took her!"

"How many guards?"

"Five."

Cinch nodded at Pan, then at Gus. "Stay here, arm yourselves. I'll find Wanita."

They'd already taken out four, that left one.

He didn't have to go far.

In a bedroom around the corner, he found the last guard, half dressed, trying to hold his pants up with one hand, and a fat-bladed hunting knife to the front of Wanita's neck with the other. Her clothes had been slit, one breast was bare, and her left eye was puffed up, a trickle of blood from the split skin next to it.

Cinch slid into a shooting crouch five meters away, his pistol locked in both hands, the sights on the guard's forehead.

"Hold it right there!" the man said. His voice cracked. He was young, maybe twenty-four or -five, and scared.

"Put the knife down and you live."

"I'll cut her goddamned throat!"

"And you'll be dead before she starts to bleed. Put the knife down." Cinch took a deep breath, let half of it out, and held the rest of the air.

"I want a ride out of here!" He pressed the edge of the knife against Wanita's throat.

"Fine. It's a deal. Put the knife down and you can leave. I don't want you, you're a little fish—"

"Fuck you, you bastard!"

Cinch saw him tense and knew the time for talk was

done. He squared his sights, put them on the man's left eye, and fired. The guard flew backward, the knife spun away as his arms went rigid, the stronger muscles of the triceps straightening them.

Cinch ran to Wanita. "You okay?"

She took a couple of deep breaths and blew them out. "Yeah. He was just getting warmed up when you got here. Hadn't done anything but smack me a couple of times."

Cinch looked at the corpse. "That was stupid. I would have let him go."

"Shouldn't have called him a little fish," she said. "I think he was sensitive about his size."

He raised an eyebrow at her.

"Well. His mighty sword kinda wilted when I laughed at how small it was."

Cinch smiled. "You're kidding, right?"

"Like hell. If I'm going to be raped, I want the bastard to suffer. If he *had* kept it up, I was going to bite it off." She paused for a second. "Everybody else okay?"

"Yeah."

"What about Tuluk?"

"We'll get to him later. He played his cards wrong and the game is all but over."

He put an arm around her and they went to find the others.

chapter 28

Tuluk's fear filled him like the water from a broken well-head fills the pit it lies in. "Call the ranch again!"

"They didn't answer the last three times, why do you think they'll answer now?"

"Just shut up and call!"

Lobang shrugged and touched a control.

No answer.

"Damn them! Why don't they respond?"

"My guess is the ranger and a bunch of Kohl's men stormed in there and shot them all to pieces while we were waiting here with our dicks in our hands to get the drop on them." Lobang chuckled.

"What do you have to laugh about, idiot? Your fortunes are tied to mine. If I fall, you'll be there to cushion it when I land!"

Lobang didn't speak to that.

"Where are you going?" Tuluk had been preoccupied. After their escape from the attack at Three Trees, he hadn't thought a lot about where Lobang was flying, just as long as it was out of immediate danger. But now . . . now he had to come up with a plan. He would have stayed and fought, hired phalanxes of lawyers to bribe and weasel through the charges—if all the rangers had was wishful thinking. But with the recordings and the witness, not to mention the kidnapping charges, things might be more

201

than he could finesse. Maybe it was time to clean out the emergency account and take a long space voyage. He had a few million tucked away for such a contingency. He never thought he'd have to use it, but maybe this was the time. He could start over, build up another fortune. It wasn't too late and he would have a head start this time, he'd already be rich by most standards. Fuck his dead father.

"Lobang? Where are we going? You want to answer me?"

The man remained silent, but in a moment the armor-tempered glass plate that sealed the passenger cab from the driver's compartment suddenly slid up from its recess in the steel frame of the seat back. It snicked shut and locked, the thick glass polarized to a dark and opaque gray.

"Lobang you asshole! What are you doing?"

Lobang didn't speak to that, either.

Tuluk's pit-of-the-belly fear turned to rage, now that he had a convenient focus. He reached for the controls in his seat arm and fingered the one that dropped the glass armor plate.

The plate did not move.

"Dammit!"

Tuluk stabbed at the window, then the door controls.

Nothing. Lobang had some kind of override up front. That wasn't supposed to be possible.

"What the hell are you doing?"

Lobang still did not answer. With the plate opaqued, they couldn't see each other.

Tuluk drew his tangler, pointed it at the glass, then thought better of it. AT glass was supposed to be able to stop most of a tangler's beam and enough of it might splash back on him to cause him real damage. Besides, if he did kill Lobang, the limo on manual as it was would crash. From this height and at this speed, even the best restraints would probably not spare him major injury or death. To be badly wounded and trapped in a crashed limo in the desert with people who wanted to find him would not be a good situation.

He didn't know what the brainless thug was up to, but that didn't look good, either.

There was a spare tangler under a floor plate. Nobody knew about it but Tuluk, he'd installed it himself. He pulled the second tangler out. It was a one-shot model, half the size of his regular weapon, something you could tuck in a belt or up a sleeve and not have anybody notice right off. He put the compact weapon into his belt at the small of his back.

Lobang had left the outside windows clear. After a few minutes, the terrain began to look familiar and Tuluk knew where they were headed:

Back to the ranch.

Lobang, the son of a bitch, was selling him out!

chapter 29

Cinch and others were headed for their transportation back to Kohl's ranch when the call came. It was direct to the ranger's com.

"Ranger? This is Anjing Lobang."

"What do you want?"

"I've got a little present for you. We'll be landing in about five minutes. Tell your troops not to open up on us."

Cinch looked at Wanita. Kohl, a few meters away, was in a deep conversation with Baji. Neither of them looked happy about it, nor had Pan been pleased to hear Cinch's conclusion regarding the young woman. He hadn't believed it, until Baji sneered at him and called him a kid who thought with his dick. Whatever was going to happen to Baji, Cinch planned to leave to Gus. She might be technically guilty of several crimes, but Cinch didn't think the rangers would worry about the details.

"What do you think he's up to?" Wanita asked. "Lobang?"

"I don't know. I have an idea, but let's wait and see."

Given that eight or ten of Kohl's men were now at the ranch, well armed and ready to blast anything that moved, Cinch figured they were in good shape.

* * *

"I'm going to open the rear window on your left side," Lobang's voice came through the intercom. "I want you to toss your tangler past my window where I can see it."

"Or else what?"

"Or else I flood the compartment with emetic gas and you puke your guts out for the next hour and a half, after which I take the tangler and shove it up your ass for making me do it. I'm not your fucking dog, Tuluk."

"It won't work, Lobang. You've been with me all along. Part of my whole operation, drugs, murder—"

"I never killed anybody."

"You tried to kill the ranger! You saw *me* kill the drug dealer and Picobe. That makes you an accessory!"

"We'll see. The tangler?"

Tuluk suppressed his anger. It wouldn't do him any good at the moment. The window went down. He stuck his arm out and tossed the tangler past the driver's window.

"Very good. Sit back and enjoy your last two minutes of freedom, M. Tuluk."

Cinch watched the limo circle and come to a soft landing ten meters away. The driver's door opened and Lobang stepped out, his hands held high, fingers spread.

"Face down," Cinch called. "Keep your hands away from your weapon."

Lobang obeyed. He laughed as he did so.

"What does he think is so fucking funny?" Wanita asked.

"I expect he'll tell us that in a minute."

One of Kohl's hands relieved Lobang of his pistol. When he was clear, Cinch said, "Okay, you can get up. Slow and easy."

The big man obeyed, still grinning. "That present I mentioned. In the backseat. The door can be opened from the outside now."

"Good. Why don't you be the one to open it." It was not a question.

Still smiling, Lobang ambled to the limo's rear compartment and opened the door.

Inside sat **Manis** Tuluk, and if looks were knives, everyone outside the limo would have been flayed to the bone.

"Why don't you step out here, M. Tuluk?" Cinch said.

"I had him toss his weapon earlier," Lobang said. "He shouldn't offer any trouble."

Cinch shook his head. Did it sound as if Lobang had picked up twenty or thirty IQ points since last they'd talked? Damn.

Cinch reflected for a moment. He knew then what he suspected was true.

Kohl came over to stand in front of Tuluk. He had a pressure bandage wrapped around his upper arm and a piggyback stupecomp pumping what it thought would best help heal him and make him feel better into a vein on the other arm. "You know Manis, I wanted to kill you for what you did to Baji, but the ranger talked me out of it. This way you get to suffer. They'll put you in jail, confiscate all your money and property, and even if you don't get lethal injection, you get all the years you have left to think about it. You'll die poor and alone in a cell. I like that better. That way, you get to suffer."

Kohl started to turn away.

It was exactly the wrong thing to say. Tuluk was going to kill the ranger, to use his one shot on him, but Kohl's little speech brought it for him instead. He might go down, but he was going to get there after Gus Fucking Kohl bit the dirt.

He snatched the compact tangler from his belt and swung it up to point at Kohl—

Cinch wasn't expecting the move but he was close enough to Kohl to shove him aside and he did so. The push moved Kohl enough so that Tuluk had to reset.

Time seemed to slow down as it did when it came to sudden life and death choices. It stretched thin, time did, like tar in hot sunshine.

Sound went away as Cinch's vision sharpened into crystalline razors, but all he could see was the tiny weapon in

Tuluk's right hand, the weapon that left ghostly trails of it-self as it moved to track Gus. . . .

Martial artists strive for a state they call *zanshin,* the space where they are aware of everything and no con-scious thought intrudes. Cinch achieved that state.

For one small part of a second he stood facing an en-emy empty-handed.

In the next part of that same second, his pistol was in his hand and he pressed the trigger. There was no sense of having reached for it or drawn it, it was just *there.*

He didn't hear the gun go off, wasn't aware of how many times he fired, but he saw dots appear on Tuluk's body and he counted them.

Six of them. *Onetwothreefourfivesix—*

Tuluk fell, still mired in slow time, and the weapon he held discharged at the ground. The dust achieved unbeliev-able cosmic patterns as the invisible beam hit it, psyche-delic designs from a wirehead's dream.

"Daddy!" he said.

When Tuluk hit the ground, time sped up and returned to normal speed.

"You asshole!" Lobang said. "Couldn't you have taken him without killing him?"

"Shut up, Iggy."

Wanita moved up to stand next to Cinch. She looked down at the body, then at the ranger. "What did you call Lobang?"

"Iggy. He's with the Intergalactic Drug Enforcement Agency."

"What?!"

"An undercover agent."

"Come on!" Pan said.

Cinch looked at the muscular man. "Did I get the right agency? You *are* Iggy, right?"

"That's right, shitstomper. And you just fucked up the best arrest I have ever made. You are going to pay for that."

"I don't believe it," Wanita said.

"My commander warned me there was interest in this

case from another agency. When I uncovered the drug operation, I figured it was IGDEA. I wasn't sure who the inside man—or woman—was until today."

"If you kept your goddamn nose out of things, there wouldn't have been all these problems," Lobang said. "I was handling things just fine."

Wanita blinked. "Why the hell didn't you tell us before it got to this point? He's a ranger, on your side!"

"When you are a deep cover op you don't tell anybody *any*thing. You never know whom you can trust."

"You let that man kill people," Kohl said.

"No. No, I didn't let him."

"No?" Pan put in. "What about Picobe? And Ulang?"

"Both done before I could stop him. I tried, but he did them before I could intervene."

"Bullshit, son, you could have had him under lock as soon as you knew about the drug operation."

Lobang shook his head. "We wanted the entire connection. If we'd bagged Tuluk then, we wouldn't have gotten the seller, found out about the distribution net." He looked at the drug seller's lover. "I'll be wanting to have a little talk with you when the shitstompers—the Stellar Rangers, that is—are done with you."

"People *died* because you didn't put him in jail when you could have," Wanita said.

Lobang shrugged. "Tuluk's people. Scum, just like he was. I'm sorry, officially, but this is the way the game is played. The ranger knows how it is. Ask him. Sometimes you have to give up the little fish to catch the big ones."

Cinch nodded. "Was that you took a shot at me and Kohl when I first got here? Put a bullet through the car's door?"

"I had to make it look good. You weren't in any real danger. I was the long-range rifle champion of my unit three years running. It would have take a bad ricochet for you to get hit."

"A risk you were willing to take," Cinch said.

"You stuck your nose into my operation. I had to protect my cover. That's how the game is played."

"So is this," Cinch said. He slammed a hard right fist

into Lobang's solar plexus. The bigger man lost his ability to breathe and bent over, clutching at his abdomen with both hands. He tried to tough it out, straighten out—

The hammer blow to the back of Lobang's skull didn't do Cinch's hand any good, nor would it do any permanent damage to the drug agent, but he felt pretty damned great about it nonetheless. The big man stretched out and hit the ground facedown. With any luck at all, he would have a broken nose to go with his headache; and if he wanted a rematch when he woke up, Cinch would be happy to oblige him.

He even let Sutera Kutjing have two good kicks to Lobang's ribs before he pulled him away. No doubt Sector HQ would get a nasty comminiqué from IGDEA about this. If they sent hard copy, Cinch would have it framed and hung on his wall when he got a place of his own.

Too bad he couldn't put Lobang's head next to it.

chapter 30

Wanita stood behind the bar, drawing a glass of Hitch. Cinch smiled at her as she slid it toward him. He looked at the glass but didn't reach for it. The pub was closed and they were alone.

"So what now?"

He shrugged. "Well. Both Tuluk and the guy who would have dealt his chem are dead. They were the main problems."

"Baji?"

"The Stellar Rangers have other things to worry about. Gus can do a better job there than we can."

"Pan will be glad to hear that, despite everything."

"The girl isn't beyond rehab. If she's lucky, she'll grow up and get past this. I hope so for Pan's sake as well as hers. I'll still put in a word for him with the rangers, if he's interested."

Wanita nodded. "And Lóbang? Or whatever his real name is?"

Cinch managed a wry smile. "He'll bitch to his bosses about the ranger who sucker-punched him but he won't make too much noise. Whatever he said about the operations, he was out of line. He could have stopped Tuluk before people started getting killed. At the very least, he was greedy, looking for a promotion-making arrest."

"Or maybe he wasn't looking for a promotion," Wanita said.

It was Cinch's turn to nod. "Yeah, I thought about that. Really big money sometimes has enough weight to crush even a good lawman's resolve. Whether Lobang went native or not, we'll never know. In the end he did turn Tuluk in."

"Could have been just to save his own ass," she said.

"Could have been. No way to tell."

Wanita wiped at the already clean bar. "Well. I guess that about covers it all, doesn't it?"

Cinch looked at her. "Almost. There's us."

She stopped wiping the bar. "What about us?"

"Well. I'm a ranger and I'm not too bad at it and not quite ready to give it up. But there's no rule against rangers having SOs or spouses."

Wanita grinned widely. "Why, Cinch Carston, what are you saying to me?"

Cinch flushed, something that still surprised him when it happened.

"Thank you," she said. "That might be one of the best offers I've ever had. But I'm a pub owner and I'm pretty good at that, too. I can't see myself tagging along behind a man who might get his ticket canceled every time he walks out the door. I think I would go crazy with worry pretty fast."

Cinch nodded, not speaking. "I understand."

"Listen, I like you, Ranger, a whole bunch. If you decide you want to become half-owner of a backwater pub on a one-rocket planet, I'd like a chance to reconsider your offer. If you get tired of being a professional hero, there's a place for you here."

They both smiled. He said, "That *is* one of the best offers I've ever had. Thank you." They both knew where they stood, and it wasn't a bad place. A little sad, maybe, but he could live with it.

"So, when do you ship out?"

"Three days."

Wanita put the bar rag down. "Well. I guess we'd better

get busy, you only have three days. I hate to think I let a man like you walk out of here under his own power."

Cinch laughed. Things were looking up.

At least one thing was, anyhow.

AVONOVA PRESENTS
AWARD-WINNING NOVELS
FROM MASTERS OF SCIENCE FICTION

WULFSYARN
by Phillip Mann   71717-4/ $4.99 US

MIRROR TO THE SKY
by Mark S. Geston   71703-4/ $4.99 US/ $5.99 Can

THE DESTINY MAKERS
by George Turner   71887-1/ $4.99 US/ $5.99 Can

A DEEPER SEA
by Alexander Jablokov   71709-3/ $4.99 US/ $5.99 Can

BEGGARS IN SPAIN
by Nancy Kress   71877-4/ $4.99 US/ $5.99 Can

FLYING TO VALHALLA
by Charles Pellegrino   71881-2/ $4.99 US/ $5.99 Can

THE CONTINUATION
OF THE FABULOUS
INCARNATIONS OF IMMORTALITY
SERIES

PIERS ANTHONY

FOR LOVE OF EVIL
75285-9/$4.95 US/$5.95 Can

AND ETERNITY
75286-7/$4.99 US/$5.99 Can